JAPANESE MAGIC

Max Preston, an American, was working for an army base in Japan, seeking out gangs who were dealing in arms. It was in the Lucky Dragon Club, in Yokohama, that Max first encountered Kitty, and from then on he was caught in her spell. But every time they met, thcy clashed head on — yet there was a mutual attraction they couldn't deny. There was also an air of mystery about Kitty, which began to pose a hidden threat . . .

Books by Louise Armstrong
in the Linford Romance Library:

HOLD ON TO PARADISE

LOUISE ARMSTRONG

---◆---

JAPANESE MAGIC

Complete and Unabridged

LINFORD
Leicester

First published in Great Britain in 1999

Originally published under the
name of 'Louise Strong'

First Linford Edition
published 2001

British Library CIP Data

Armstrong, Louise
    Japanese magic.—Large print ed.—
Linford romance library
1. Love stories
2. Large type books
I. Title
823.9′14 [F]

ISBN 0–7089–5974–1

Published by
F. A. Thorpe (Publishing)
Anstey, Leicestershire

Set by Words & Graphics Ltd.
Anstey, Leicestershire
Printed and bound in Great Britain by
T. J. International Ltd., Padstow, Cornwall

This book is printed on acid-free paper

1

Being inconspicuous is difficult at the best of times for a man who is over six foot six inches tall, but it's almost impossible for an American of that size to blend into the scenery in Yokohama, Japan. Nevertheless, Max Preston was doing his best to stay out of sight.

He shifted his long limbs restlessly. His legs were hopelessly cramped in the tiny Japanese car he used for surveillance work. But the car sat unobtrusively in its parking space, and hardly any of the passing crowds of this exotic port city ever gave his run-of-the-mill car a first glance, and that suited Max Preston just fine.

Right at this moment, apart from the autumn cold, his main problem was boredom. It was late at night, or early in the morning now, and even Yokohama was settling down for the night. Neon lights clicked off along the strip and the pavements were blocked with the bulging, smelly, black garbage sacks that the late workers put out as they left.

The Lucky Dragon Club was still open, and as long as it was open, Max Preston would sit there, watching the entrance from his hiding place across the cold, narrow street. His eyes were as alert as a hawk's as he waited for any sign of movement from the rats he was stalking.

The sharp clicking of heels made him look up. It was just a routine glance. His quarry was male, so he didn't expect to be interested in a female, especially not the bar hostesses who frequented this part of town. But then his jaw dropped in surprise.

The redhead he was looking at was gorgeous, but not in any nightclub kind of way. Her short coat was wool, and it was wrapped around her warmly. There was no lipstick on her wide, dreamy lips. The hem of a long, pink, rose-printed cotton skirt dipped and swirled around her ankles. The ankles were slender and attractive, Max noted, but they ended in sensible, low-heeled shoes.

The woman he was eyeing — her heels had stopped clicking now, and she was peering around her uncertainly from under a soft, wild mass of auburn corkscrew curls — was not the kind of woman he associated with the Lucky Dragon Club. She was nice, he approved mentally. She looked as if she would be pleasantly curved in all the right places. He hated skinny women.

There was something so attractive about the thought of a sweetly curved woman. She would be soft, and yield pleasantly when a man put his arms around her, Max mused. Then, although his eyes were still glued longingly on the girl, who was scrabbling in her shoulder bag, he gave himself a mighty shake.

Since being assigned to operations in the East, he hadn't even dated. Why was he thinking about women now? The redhead he was watching screwed up her eyes and squinted at the piece of paper she had taken out of her bag. The map, or whatever it was, didn't seem to help her. She took a few hesitant steps forward, looking around her uncertainly.

Max shook his head. Japan is one of the most civilised countries on earth, and generally a woman can walk safely alone through its streets, but even the most delightful of cities has its pockets of vice and sin, and this area was Yokohama's.

The street of the Lucky Dragon Club was no place for a woman alone, not unless she was a trained commando! But he'd bet his favourite rifle that this little lady was nothing of the sort. She had a kind of sweet, but dizzy air about her that made Max want to rush over and protect her.

For the second time he shook himself mentally. Whatever was he thinking about? The rules of surveillance were strict and simple — an operative didn't reveal himself, ever, not for any reason, not even for an appealing little lady in a soft grey coat with a band of white fluff around the hood that pooled around her ears like a collar.

'Whoa, boy!' Max muttered aloud trying to get control of his wayward mind. He deliberately thought back to his surveillance training. He remembered his instructor's words.

'You gotta beware of women. They'll try and get you, but you don't fall for it, ever. If a naked babe walks by, you assume she's with the enemy! The first and last rule of covert operations is to stay under cover.'

'Yes, sir! Ignore the babes!' Max muttered, as if he was answering his old teacher.

He knew how good that advice was. This was an important operation. His unit had been setting it up for months. They were on the trail of an international gang selling stolen military weapons to any two-bit dictator with the money.

Max checked the dark street. He shifted uneasily in the cramped, cold, little car. This was serious business, and he wasn't about to be distracted from the job by enticing visions of a woman's tempting lips and appealing eyes, all soft and delicious.

'You're doing it again!' Max scolded himself.

He was glad when the redhead seemed to come to a decision. She gathered her coat around her and walked away rapidly. Max listened to her sharp heel clicks fading and told himself he was glad that she had gone. Now he could concentrate on the cold, dark street and the serious and lonely business of tracking down criminals.

But instead of feeling glad, Max suddenly realised how cold and bored and lonely he was. He looked at his watch. Another three hours before he was relieved. He rubbed his cold nose. He shifted his cramped position. He yawned and cracked his finger joints.

And then the footsteps came again, click, click, clicking back towards him. Max felt a huge smile lifting the corners of his mouth.

Anything to break the boredom, he told himself hastily. It's not that I have any special interest in this dame. Not at all. Of course, I should watch her carefully. Could be she isn't as innocent as she looks if she's going into that den of thieves.

Yellow light from the doors of the Lucky Dragon Club backlit the halo of red curls as the little lady trotted up the entrance steps. She stopped by the giant, carved ebony dragon that coiled around the front of the club. A crimson bulb inside the head of the dragon made its eyes glow ruby red. Max groaned in disbelief as she stopped to pat the dragon's nose.

'She's as flaky as a Maryland cookie,' he muttered.

Then things began to happen fast. Light and music spilled out into the dark street as an oriental hostess with an exotic orchid pinned into her glossy black chignon burst through the door of the Lucky Dragon Club, slamming it hard behind her. A thick-set, beefy man in a dinner jacket opened the door again, threw a fluffy white jacket and little gold purse down the steps after the hostess, and slammed the door once more.

The redhead Max had been watching stepped back out of the way as the hostess picked up the white fluffy jacket and brushed it off with sharp, angry movements. The exotic woman didn't pick up the gold purse. She kicked it disdainfully with the toe of her gleaming patent-leather spike-heeled shoe. Then, sequins glittering, she tossed her head, charged down the steps and stalked down the centre of the narrow street. Within seconds, her elegant figure was swallowed up in the shadows.

Max's redhead moved forward hesitantly and picked up the discarded purse. She looked at it doubtfully, then made a tentative move towards the door of the Lucky Dragon Club. From behind her, a crouching black figure burst out of the shadows, ran up the club steps, and grabbed at her hand, the one holding the gold purse.

Max tensed, but his duty was clear. He could not risk blowing such an important cover operation to get involved in a petty case of bag snatching. Yet his hands clenched, and a murderous rage swept him. His whole body trembled as his military training battled with his primitive desire to leap out of the car and protect that sweet and charming lady.

Then he leaned forward in surprise. A muffled cheer escaped him.

'Go for it, babe!'

The words burst through his lips, but his training kept them in a choked whisper. She was fighting back like a wildcat. She swung the gold purse on its length of chain like a mediaeval weapon, forcing the attacker's head back. Her sturdy shoes lashed out at the man's ankles, catching him off balance. Her nails flashed in the air like razors.

Max could tell by the way she moved that she had never had a combat lesson in her life, but she had enough fighting spirit in that tiny frame to power a whole boatload of commandos! And the attacker was down!

'Yes!' Max hissed, wanting to shout out loud, but still remembering that he was supposed to stay out of sight.

He punched the air. He felt proud of her.

'Now, run for it,' he urged her. 'Get away while your enemy is down.'

Panting and tossing those ridiculous curls back, the girl did take a few steps away. Then Max heard new footsteps as a large figure in jeans and white roll-neck sweater marched quickly out of the shadows towards the mêlée on the steps of the nightclub. His appearance was definitely nautical. The blonde rushed up to him.

The sailor had olive skin and black hair that could have belonged to any nationality, but his massive build spoke of western beef and a well-fed childhood. Unconsciously Max relaxed. The marines were here. Now his brave little lady would have the help she deserved.

'Quick!' she cried, brandishing the gold purse in the sailor's face, then swinging round to point at the writhing figure on the steps behind her. 'That man tried to steal this purse. Please, help me!'

Even raised to a shout, her voice was attractive, and Max heard her cut-glass accent with surprise.

'A Brit!' he said to himself. 'Well, I'll be darned.'

Then Max's attention focused sharply on the sailor. The man had pulled a knife. Its blade glittered in the cold air. What the heck? Max frowned, his hand reaching for the door handle of the car. Something was wrong here. The sailor was pointing the knife directly at the little lady!

'Help you, lady? That's a laugh!'

the sailor growled, gesturing at the sprawled figure of the redhead's attacker. 'I'm helping him! Now just give me the purse and no-one will get hurt.'

Max's reflexes acted for him. He drew his gun. No-one should have to face odds like that alone. She'd fought like a good 'un and look what fate had done to her! He wasn't going to stand for it.

Hinges groaning, the car door burst open. Max hit the ground rolling. He lifted the gun, aiming for the dull glitter of the knife. The girl was well out of his line of fire, but his firearms training made Max shout, 'Girlie! Down! Get out of the way!'

With her conscious mind, Katherine Morland heard the shouting only as a confused noise. She had a lot else to think about just then. Luckily, her subconscious mind knew the voice of a hero when it heard one, and it listened to his commands and decided to obey them. Her knees were like rubber, anyway, in reaction to the shock of the evening's events. It took very little to propel her body forward on to the pavement.

A gun cracked above her head. A heavy, bulky figure hit her from behind. She caught a whiff of the most delicious male aftershave. A large, hot body pinned her to the cold, dirty road.

'Keep your head down!' a voice hissed in her ear.

The voice set up vibrations that shivered all the way from the nape of her neck to the base of her spine. Mmm! A deep American drawl — her favourite accent!

Her favourite accent! What was she doing, thinking about accents when she was pinned to the ground and there were maniacs with guns and knives all around her? Katherine Morland, known to one and all as Kitty, struggled to take in a breath and make sense of the world.

Only half an hour ago, she had been comfortably ensconced in a delightful

Japanese restaurant, munching morsels of delicious grilled meat, and titbits like toasted mushrooms and nuts. Her mouth watered as she thought of the tasty food. And her hosts had been so sweet! She had been with six attentive students from her English class for businessmen. They had treated her like a princess, waiting on her hand and foot. And now look at her, pinned to the ground in a Yokohama backstreet!

If only Mr Tanaka hadn't left his wallet behind. If only she hadn't tried to follow him, so that she could return the wretched thing! If only she hadn't taken a wrong turning, or five or six wrong turnings. Why hadn't she waited until tomorrow to track down Mr Tanaka? Why did she always land in a scrape?

Although her ears were still ringing from the gunshot, Kitty could hear running footsteps as her assailants fled. Her rescuer gave a sigh of relief. The heavy weight that was pinning her down eased up. She wanted to turn around to look at him, but an iron hand on her upper arm prevented her from moving. A deep voice tickled her ear.

'You OK?'

Kitty drew in a shaky breath.

'Yes, I think so.'

Again that gorgeous rumble.

'You did well there, lady, real good. You hit the first one of those thieves like a tornado.'

From out of the darkness of the street, a cautious voice shouted a question in Japanese. The large body behind her stiffened when he heard it.

'Listen, lady, the police will be here any minute, and I shouldn't be. So take care now!'

The sensation of leaning against a vast, comforting man mountain went away. Kitty lifted herself and looked after him, but all she could see was a large, muscular shadow, running lightly into the dark of the night.

'Wait!' she called. 'I didn't even say thank you!'

But he was gone.

2

So I legged it,' Kitty said cheerfully, as she finished recounting the previous night's adventures to her American friend and colleague, Candy.

They were taking a coffee break in the intimate, elegant coffee shop near the English language school where Kitty worked at night to fund her morning ikebana classes. She and Candy had gotten into the habit of coffee-housing together before the evening lessons began.

'You ran away? You didn't wait for the police?' Candy asked, her eyes as large as the delicate bone china saucer before her.

'What could I tell them?' Kitty asked, taking a sip of her cappuccino. 'I'm a florist, not a secret agent. I didn't know what was going on. I didn't see anyone's face. I couldn't describe anyone.'

She paused, listening to the light, bright music that was spilling over the café's sound system. Here in this sunny coffee house, with an orchid on every table and Mozart lifting her heart, she couldn't believe in the dark events of the night before.

'Was your purse stolen? Did you lose anything?' Candy asked.

Kitty couldn't help smiling.

'Far from it. I gained three items over the course of the evening, including Mr Tanaka's wallet, which is what originally got me into the mess. I've arranged for it to go to his office by motorcycle messenger.'

'That's efficient, honey,' Candy said.

She lifted her cake fork and sliced lovingly into a slice of maple walnut chocolate cake. She was just lifting the fork to her mouth when she noticed Kitty's face.

'Hey, what did I say to upset you?'

For a moment Kitty didn't want to tell her. A curious feeling twisted in her stomach. Then she gathered her courage. She lifted her chin, drew in a deep breath and tried to make her voice sound casual.

'Oh, it's just that my ex-boyfriend doesn't share your opinion.'

Then she swallowed. It was difficult to go on. She occupied herself with stirring her coffee.

'Ex!' Candy screamed. 'Are you telling me you have split up with that heavenly diplomat? How could you, Kitty? He was just divine!'

'He wasn't that heavenly, and it was he who did the splitting, actually,' Kitty said, but Candy continued to rant.

'You manage to find a gorgeous, eligible male and you let him go?'

'He wasn't all that wonderful, and it was he who let me go,' Kitty pointed out once more.

She felt a little, a very little, better. Talking about unpleasant things seemed to cut them down to size. He hadn't been special with her, but being assessed, and found wanting, always hurt.

'Why did he let you go?' Candy demanded. 'What happened? Was the party on Saturday a disaster? Oh, Kitty, don't tell me it all went wrong. I was looking forward to some glamorous living by proxy with my friend going to a ball at the British Embassy.'

'Oh, no, she didn't,' Kitty said. 'The ball was the night before I thought it was, Friday night not Saturday night, and he was furious that I got it all mixed up.'

'You got the dates wrong! Kitty! How could you do that? You forgot to go to Prince Diplomat's ball!'

'He wasn't very diplomatic about me,' Kitty replied, wincing as she remembered the biting fluency of his assassination of her character.

'What did he say?' Candy probed.

'The same things every man in my life seems to say, just before walking out, that I'm too chaotic, too disorganised, too lightweight, too frivolous, oh, a whole boring list of things. I should have realised when he gave me that organiser diary last month that we were headed for disaster.'

'Couldn't you have used it for him?' Candy demanded, but then she seemed to remember female solidarity. 'Of course, you're perfect as you are, Kitty, but you could have made a little effort for a desirable male like the diplomat.'

Suddenly Candy noticed the mess she was making of her piece of cake as she talked. She began to clear it up with a paper napkin, laughing at herself the while.

'Oh, look at me, trying to give you advice! I think you should stay in Japan instead of going home to open a flower shop. We could turn into two dotty, old English teachers together. I know you want to teach Japanese flower arranging, but you're a great English teacher, too. That reminds me. There's a bouquet of flowers waiting for you in reception. Yoko Tanaka passed her exams, all thanks to you, she says, and she's been offered a place at Oxford University, all thanks to you, she says.'

'I didn't have to do anything special. She was a good student,' Kitty said as they got up to go.

As they collected up their purses, gloves, scarves and bags full of teaching papers, Kitty was glad that Candy couldn't question her further about the two other items she had gained last night, because she didn't quite know what to do with them herself.

She continued to turn the problem over in the back of her mind all the way through the classes she taught that evening, and all the way through her dreams that night, but by the next afternoon, she had decided what to do about one of the items at least.

★   ★   ★

The guard on the gate of the military base looked at Kitty as if she was subnormal.

'Ma'am, I can't tell you the names of our officers.'

Kitty repeated patiently, 'I don't want

you to tell me the names of all your officers. I want you to tell me if you have one officer, called Max Preston, stationed in Japan. I don't want any military secrets.'

'Ma'am, I can't tell you that.'

'Just say yes or no. That's all I need.'

The soldier stared solidly ahead.

'I can't do that, ma'am.'

Kitty bit her lip in frustration and squinted at the watch in her hand. The autumn sunlight glinted off its gun-metal case and broken watch strap.

'I just need to know if you have a Max Preston. Then I can return this watch that he dropped while he was, uh, helping me.'

'Ma'am, it's against regulations to tell you anything.'

Kitty shook her head in exasperation. She just wanted to know if she could safely leave Max Preston's watch at the gatehouse and know it would reach him.

Following the principle of going straight to the top, Kitty had brought the watch to the Tokyo headquarters of the American army, but now they wouldn't take it! She felt like giving up her attempt to do this good deed, but she also felt a sense of obligation towards the watch owner, because after all, he must have lost it while he was rescuing her.

She looked at the guard wondering what she could say to make him help her. He continued to stare solidly at the toes of his extremely large boots. It was difficult to say which of them was the most relieved when a man with a very pleasant face marched over and broke the impasse.

'Trouble, corporal?' he demanded sternly, but he gave Kitty a reassuring smile.

'Not exactly, sir,' the guard said, stuttering nervously as he explained the situation.

Kitty studied the newcomer, admiring his relaxed but alert stance as he heard the guard out. Judging by the newcomer's gold braid and medals, he was very senior indeed. Once he was satisfied that he had the gist of the situation he turned to Kitty and said, 'What makes you think that the man who lost this watch is an American soldier?' he asked.

Her hands went to the crystal she wore on a fine gold chain on her neck. An image of the crystal spinning over a map of Tokyo flashed into her mind, but she knew she couldn't share that kind of experience with anyone who was practical enough to hold down a job that required a uniform. They would never believe her.

Kitty wouldn't lightly discuss her ability to gain information through the use of a crystal pendulum with her close friends, let alone two macho-looking soliders, but she trusted the knowledge that came to her through the crystal. As soon as the crystal had come to rest, not over Tokyo, but farther down the coast, directly over the town where the military base was, she had known it was right. Where else would an action hero with a delicious American drawl appear from?

The senior officer was still waiting for an answer. Kitty blinked up at him.

'Actually, I got the impression that he's stationed on one of your bases, rather than in Tokyo.'

She hoped he wouldn't notice that she hadn't answered his question directly. The senior officer gave her another keen glance, but he smiled at her kindly.

'Why don't you leave the watch along with your name and address? If we have any problems returning the item, we'll contact you.'

Kitty fished in her overflowing shoulder bag until she found one of the business cards her school issued her with. It was printed in English on one side and in elegant oriental writing on the other side. She still got a kick out of seeing her name in Japanese. The officer took her card and the watch and smiled at her.

'Regulations don't allow us to give

out information on service personnel, but I'm sure someone will be glad to see this watch again.'

He looked at Kitty's card and then turned the battered watch over and looked at the inscription.

'Yes, ma'am, I'm sure that Max Preston will be contacting you any day now to express his gratitude.'

I don't suppose he will contact me, Kitty thought wistfully as she walked down the hill away from the military offices and towards the train station. As she got on the train, Kitty pictured once more the warm, powerful figure and the American accent that had sent shivers down her spine. Then she scolded herself severely.

I'll have to stop thinking about Max Preston or I'll be in trouble, she decided. Besides, he won't call me. He might be glad to get his watch back, but he'll probably never give me another thought.

How wrong she was, but she was quite unaware of the effect getting back his watch had on Max Preston.

'There's nothing for it,' he said to one of his colleagues. 'I'll have to contact this Katherine Morland and interrogate her.'

'Take it easy, Max,' his team-mate warned. 'There's just a chance she could be no more than an innocent civilian.'

'Impossible! There's no way an innocent civilian could have traced me. She has to be in it up to her pretty, little ears.'

He felt a curious pang of regret as he spoke. He brushed it away and looked at the man standing before the blackboard in the briefing room.

'I just wish that you could deal with her, John. You're the ladies' man around here.'

His Australian colleague laughed.

'It might be good for you to get involved with a woman for a change. How long is it since you even dated?'

Max thought back. His work kept him in a very male-orientated world, and so busy that he had no time to go looking for female company. It wasn't unless they made an effort that women crossed Max's path.

'Too long,' Max said with a sigh. 'And that's what worries me. I don't know what tricks the little lady's gonna try on me, and I'm 'way out of practice.'

'You'll be a match for her,' another of the team said comfortingly. 'Forewarned is forearmed. You know she must be with the gang. You know she'll be after information. They can't know the scale of this operation, but they may be beginning to suspect we're after them. It's difficult to keep so many people under observation for so long and not have them spot you.'

'That would be right,' John said. 'Something's spooked them all right, and smugglers tend towards paranoia. My bet is this female's been set up to trap you.'

'We can use that to our advantage,' another said. 'Pretend to fall for it,

Max, and convince them that no-one is after them.'

'I'm a soldier, not a spy,' Max grumbled. 'Why don't I just go around there and shake her until she tells us the truth?'

3

Kitty was wandering around the deserted school dreamily straightening plants and putting stray books away when she saw the shadow in the doorway. Some of the female teachers didn't like locking up as it meant being alone in the empty building, but Kitty had never been afraid, until now.

'Who's there?' she called sharply.

The shadow moved, grew larger, and resolved itself into a broad-chested, broad-shouldered mountain of a man. Kitty stared at him with a dry mouth. She didn't need the faint tang of lemon and cinnamon aftershave to tell her who this was!

'Katherine Morland?' he inquired.

'Yes.'

Her voice sounded like a faint squeak compared to the gorgeous liquid rumble of his.

'I believe I have to thank you for the return of my watch.'

Another faint squeak, 'Yes,' escaped her lips.

He moved a little closer to her, and she shrank back, not quite knowing why. He was, after all, the most gorgeous man she had ever seen in her life.

He looked fit for anything that required a well-muscled man. He carried an aura of power and alert fighting readiness. He was wearing crisp denims and a cable-knit jersey with the precision of a uniform. He was clean shaven, and his dark hair was immaculately groomed. Kitty experienced an inexplicably strong desire to run her hands through its thickness.

Then she looked into his eyes, and she realised why she had stepped back. His eyes were not friendly at all. Dark, treacle-toffee eyes glared at her through cold, narrow slits.

'How on earth did you know how to find me?' he snapped.

'I'm sorry,' Kitty said automatically, responding to his tone.

He scowled down at her.

'Never mind, I'm sorry. Just tell me what you hope to get out of this.'

Kitty flushed. I'm rapidly going off this man, she thought.

Aloud, she said, aware that her voice was still not quite steady, 'I don't know what you mean. All I wanted to do was return your watch.'

He lifted a dark, well-shaped eyebrow.

'And leave your address so I'd contact you?'

His glare seemed to suggest that he thought he'd scored a point there. Kitty thought ruefully of the lovely dream she'd had last night. She had been walking through drifts of autumn leaves in a Japanese temple garden with her mystery hero.

You should always meet the man before you start dreaming about him, Kitty, she told herself. Crocodile wrestling is more this man's kind of weekend, and I don't like him.

'The guard at the gatehouse wouldn't accept the watch unless I left identification,' she explained. 'I wasn't expecting any response from you. I was just following military procedure.'

Far from pacifying him, her answer made his scowl even deeper.

'What do you know about military procedure?'

When he breathed in, the room seemed to shrink and he seemed to grow larger, looming over Kitty. But Kitty was beginning to collect her wits and feel angry. Who did this man think he was, barging into the school and growling at her?

'I don't know anything about it, and if you are following military procedure by responding to my returning your watch by yelling at me and scaring me halfway into next week, then I don't want to know anything about it, either.'

She expected him to leave, but instead he just folded his arms and glared down at her. He really did have the most gorgeous body! It was wasted on this horrible bully.

His mouth twisted and he snarled, 'If you are so innocent, lady, how come you knew where to find me?'

Kitty's hands went to the crystal at her throat.

'I, uh, I . . . '

'I'm waiting,' he snapped.

'Well, I can't remember.'

He shifted his weight from one foot to the other.

'Who told you where to find me?'

'No-one!' she said indignantly. 'And what does it matter?'

'It matters because I don't aim on leaving here until you tell me.'

She just knew that this wasn't the kind of man to appreciate what she was going to say, but it was the only way to get rid of him. She held out her crystal for his inspection.

'I have a kind of talent for finding lost things, or people. I use this crystal as a pendulum.'

She sneaked a glance at his face

through her lashes. The scowl had deepened until it was black. Her voice shook as she went on.

'I held the pendulum over a map, and it came to rest over the military base. It made sense to me, so I took your watch to the gatehouse, and, and here we are — just getting on like a house on fire.'

He was still growing bigger every time he took in a breath. His eyes were cold brown lasers and his lips twisted in disgust.

'Oh, what do you take me for, lady? Are you going to tell me the truth, or am I going to have to shake it out of you?'

'That is the truth!' Kitty squealed. 'And how dare you threaten me like that! I'm not one of your tin soldiers, you know. You can't push me around like that.'

He lifted a cool eyebrow.

'No?'

'No!' she yelled. 'And now you are making me really angry.'

And really worried about the empty

school, her thoughts ran. Would anyone hear me if I screamed? She had to get rid of him.

'I don't know what you're accusing me of or why! I'm sorry I returned your watch. I'm sorry I did you a favour. If there is anything else you'd like me to apologise for, I will. Anything, so long as it gets you out of here.'

'I'm not leaving until you tell me just what you were hoping to achieve by engineering this meeting,' he thundered.

'How can you be so arrogant?' Kitty gasped. 'I didn't want to meet you. All I did was return your watch! It is normal behaviour, you know, to return lost items to their owners.'

He glared at her. His arms were still folded. How could he look so menacing while remaining completely still?

'However those said owners are tracked down,' she continued feebly.

His toffee-brown eyes still glared. Kitty swallowed nervously. She tried to make her tone flippant.

'I don't know what else military procedure recommends doing with a lost watch — using it for target practice, perhaps?'

'Less of your lip, lady,' he growled. 'Just tell me how you found me.'

'Less of your bullying, action man,' she replied, glaring right back at him.

Was that a gleam of respect she saw in the depths of his treacle-toffee eyes? She followed up her advantage.

'Your name was on the watch. You had an American accent. You carried a gun. The American army has personnel stationed here. How many beans make five?'

'Sarcastic, aren't you?' he grumbled.

'Stupid,' Kitty said, getting into her stride, 'and unlucky. Of all the heroes in all the world, I have to get rescued by this one. Mister, if I say thank you for rescuing me from the guy with the carving knife, will you leave now?'

'Nope. And it was a switchblade knife, not a carving knife.'

'That's repetition,' Kitty snapped.

An eyebrow raised.

'A switchblade is a knife, so why say switchblade and knife?' Kitty explained sweetly. 'Or is it military procedure to say everything twice? I think I've heard on the news that troops prepare in advance, assemble together, advance ahead, and then make violent explosions that level the enemy to the ground. All repetition, you'll agree.'

Her attack left him unruffled.

'Regulations say we have to be clear in all our communications. And what I need to be clear about in my mind is just exactly what you were doing outside the Lucky Dragon Club.'

A wave of pure fury hit Kitty. Just who did he think he was! She'd explained, she'd apologised, she'd even tried teasing him, and he was still grilling her like they were in a third-rate war movie. She'd had enough.

'I was meeting my lover, the notorious criminal, Wing Fat Lee,' she explained sarcastically. 'By day, I'm an innocent English teacher, by night, I slip into my alter ego, that of Kitten Cat Bond, femme fatale and international spy.'

She couldn't believe it — he was nodding in satisfaction!

'Kitten,' he said. 'It suits you. Now, Kitten, how long have you known Wing Fat Lee?'

Completely exasperated, she screamed with the full force of her lungs.

'Are you out of your mind?'

He looked puzzled.

'What? It's no good getting coy about it. If you don't tell me the details someone else will.'

Kitty was almost snorting in her exasperation.

'How could you possibly think I'm having an affair with a man out of a comic book?'

He ran lazy eyes over her.

'You're not his usual type, true, but I can see the attraction.'

Kitty fell back in disbelief. She felt as if all her clothes had melted away under his look. His eyes were hot and stripping. They held a sensual, appraising gleam that made her feel uncomfortable and breathless.

She took three deep breaths and began to edge around his massive body. He made no move to stop her, but swivelled his whole frame in a scanning motion, like a security camera, so that he kept her in his sight. Kitty made a dart to the reception desk and picked up her coat with trembling hands. Her coat suddenly seemed to have lost an armhole and turned itself inside out.

'Allow me.'

Shudders zinged down her spine as the man-mountain who had just been tormenting her took the coat from her fumbling hands and wrapped it around her shoulders. It galled her that she had to allow him to help her. She was quiveringly aware of his large, musky male body looming large above her.

Once her coat was on, she twisted away from him and pulled the folds of grey wool around her as if they were armour. She picked up the keys to the school as if they were a weapon. Then she darted across the reception area to stand by the double glass doors that led in and out of the school. Right next to the doors was the electronic alarm system. Kitty put her hand on it, staring defiantly into the melting brown eyes of her interrogator.

'Out!' she said grimly. 'I've had enough of you. I tell you the truth and you threaten me. I tell you a story out of Dick Tracy and you believe me! I want you out of here.'

His smile was mocking, taunting.

'And if I don't choose to go?'

Kitty drew in a shaky, but determined breath.

'Then I set off the alarms.'

He gave her a long, hard measuring look that wasn't without respect.

'I can see you mean it. OK, Kitten, no need to wave your little claws at me. I'm going. Now I've got the truth out of you, some other guy will fill me in on all the details of your little affair with Wing Fat Lee.'

'There is no Wing Fat Lee,' Kitty almost snarled.

'I can understand that it's the kind of connection you wouldn't like anyone at school to know about,' Max commented drily. 'But there's only us chickens here, so why not spill the beans, Kitten?'

'And my name is not Kitten!'

'It's a cute, little name for a cute, little lady! I can just see you working in Wing Fat's restaurant dressed as a French maid!'

His eyes slid lazily over Kitty's face and neck. Her eyes met his with a sharp click, and she got some idea of the thoughts that were crossing his mind. She gathered her slipping dignity.

'Out!' she hissed. 'I never want to talk to you or see you again.'

'Shame,' Max said, laughing in a way that brought the blood up under her cheeks. 'I'd love to see you in a black mini skirt. I bet your legs are terrific.'

Kitty's hand trembled on the alarm. She was ready to let it rip, but he unfolded his arms, shifted his big body and sauntered past her as coolly as if he were going for a seaside stroll.

'So long, Kitten Kat,' he said amiably.

Kitty's lips lifted in an involuntary snarl as he went by. He tilted his head over his shoulder and laughed at her response openly.

'Or should I say Tiger?'he mocked.

He ignored the elevator, and his laughter floated up to her with his footsteps as he loped out of sight down the bare, echoing stairs. Kitty was now trembling so much that she nearly set the alarms off by accident, but eventually she got the school locked up and was able to take the lift down to the street. A tiny crescent moon sparkled in the dark blue sky.

The evening bustle of the shopping street was comforting.

Did all that really happen, Kitty wondered, standing stock still in the middle of the street. Why do I feel so strange? She took a few deep breaths and began to walk on unsteady legs. A fine, nervous trembling ran through her whole body. She looked into the brightly-lit window of the tea merchant's shop as she tottered past it. All the colours seemed brighter than normal.

Kitty absently looked at the wooden crate covered in Chinese writing. Her nerves hummed as if she had drunk too much of the black smoky tea inside it. Adrenaline? A fight or flight reaction? It wouldn't be surprising after the fright that monster had just given her!

It must be adrenaline that was making her feel so strange. The wobbly knees, the fluttering around her heart, the trembling hands? What else could it be? She felt restless and uneasy. She began walking but her body kept responding in the strangest way. What had he done to her?

Maybe she should phone the military base and complain. But if Max Preston behaved like a homicidal maniac when she did him a favour, what would he do if she complained?

Maybe she'd better not complain. Maybe she'd better just put the whole thing out of her mind.

4

Back at the base, Max Preston was lying on his bare army cot in his bare army room staring at the ceiling. He heaved a deep sigh and his head moved restlessly on the arms that were crossed behind him on the flat pillow. His thoughts were uncomfortable to say the least. He felt as if he had failed in his mission to discover the truth about Kitty's involvement with the gang they were tailing.

He hadn't failed to notice the admiration in her misty blue eyes when he first arrived at her school, and he'd been human enough to enjoy it, and human enough to feel sorry when that admiration turned to disappointment and anger. Why had he been so aggressive with her?

He shifted restlessly again as he remembered the scorn and defiance on her pretty little face. It had been bad tactics to scare her like that. She seemed to have an open and confiding manner. Who knows how much valuable information she might have given him if he had been friendly and won her confidence?

Max turned over and thumped the pillow. He'd failed in his mission. That was surely why he felt so uncomfortable. It was clearly his duty to seek Kitty out once more and repair the damage. He could take her to a nice restaurant for dinner, and then, when she was smiling at him again, he could doublecheck her story and find out how much more she knew about this international smuggling gang.

It was his duty to make friends with the charming, dizzy, delightful redhead, Max decided. It wasn't that he wanted to see her again, date her, anything like that. Oh, no! It was just that it was plainly his duty to see her again, that was all. He'd get her home address from the base computer in the morning.

Feeling better, Max snapped out the light and went to sleep.

★ ★ ★

Kitty was humming to herself as the sun poured in through the wide-open screens of her room in the Japanese-style student residence. She'd had a delightful morning. Her teacher in Japanese floral arranging had actually nodded in approval over Kitty's arrangement of autumn leaves and berries, and then the post had brought a lovely long letter from home, full of news about all the family. Her mother had enclosed a photograph, too, and Kitty had propped it up on her low Japanese table.

She glanced over at the smiling faces of her family. They had posed for the snapshot in the middle of the family ritual of gathering the apples that grew in the orchard of their rambling

Yorkshire home. Kitty missed them all dreadfully, but she was loving the experience of being in Japan. She knew that her course in the art of ikebana, Japanese flower arranging, would help her career.

And I'll be back with them all next year, she reminded herself. A smile curved her lips as she imagined the flower shop she intended to open in the lovely old city of York, and the ikebana course she planned to teach at the college where she had trained as a florist.

Kitty loved working with flowers and greenery. Even now she was gently tending a beautifully-shaped, but ailing, bonsai tree that a fussy neighbour had cast aside. The pottery dish that had originally housed the miniature maple tree had cracked right across. Kitty took the tree out on to her portion of the balcony terrace that ran around the building and rummaged around in the florist's supplies that she always seemed to accumulate wherever she went, but she had no flowerpots of the right shape. Then she gave a huge smile.

'Another problem solved,' she muttered to the tree, and went back into her room to pick up the gold evening bag that had got her into so much trouble in Yokohama the other night.

The bag had been troubling Kitty. What should she do with it? Seen by daylight, it was torn and grubby. She couldn't imagine anyone wanting it back, or going to the trouble of stealing it. The would-be thieves on the steps of the Lucky Dragon Club had probably made a mistake, because there was nothing worth snatching inside the bag either.

Kitty had opened it cautiously, expecting diamonds perhaps or stolen plans, or a gun at least, but it was empty save for a puzzling, dish-shaped piece of polished metal. She hadn't quite liked to throw the dish away, but given the trouble that had followed her attempts to return Mr Tanaka's wallet and then Max Preston's watch, Kitty didn't feel like making an effort to contact the owner, even supposing she could ever find one. Now she had the perfect compromise. The shallow, dish-shaped bowl would make a lovely container for her bonsai tree.

'And if anyone should come asking for it, they can have it with pleasure,' Kitty said, patting compost around the roots of the maple tree. 'But I don't think they will.'

She set the little bonsai tree in a sunny position on her terrace and gave it a long drink of water. It looked attractive in its new bowl and Kitty gave a satisfied nod.

'There you look beautiful now,' she said, smiling happily.

'I could say the same about you!' a deep voice came from right next to her.

Kitty whirled. Her heart thudded in her chest and she gave vent to her feelings with a sharp scream.

'Oh! How dare you!' she cried indignantly, glaring up at the toffee-coloured eyes that were smiling into hers.

'How dare you walk right in without knocking! You scared me to death.'

She might have recognised Max Preston right away, but she was still furious with him.

'Get out!' she screeched, too angry to debate whether the balcony terrace counted as private property or not.

Much to her surprise, Max flushed a dull red and retreated back through the washing machines and dustbins that lined the tiled area. But he didn't go away. Kitty heard the front door of the boarding house open and footsteps in the hall as Max Preston entered the building officially. He knocked firmly on the wooden sliding door to her room.

'Please may I come in?'

Kitty pressed her hands to her thudding heart and wondered what to do. Her heart felt as if it were trying to escape from her rib cage and her knees were trembling so much that it was difficult to stand up. Her reaction must be because of the fright Max had given her, creeping up on her and scaring her to death! Max knocked commandingly again on the door.

'Go away! I'm busy,' she shouted.

'Please, Kitty. I'm sorry I startled you. Let me in and I'll start all over again.'

Kitty felt herself relenting.

'What do you want?' she asked suspiciously. 'I'm not letting you in if you're going to shout at me again.'

A dcep and reassuringly attractive chuckle could be heard.

'No shouting.'

Kitty took a few steps across the matting that covered the floor of her tiny room and slid open the door, just a crack. She peered at Max suspiciously through the tiny gap.

'Then what have you come for?'

He was looking particularly handsome in an olive-coloured T-shirt and army-issue pants. His eyes lit up with a smile that took her breath away.

'Let me in and I'll tell you.'

Kitty simply could not resist a man

who smiled at her like that. She took a shaky breath and slid the door fully open. She noticed that Max had conformed to the Japanese custom and taken his boots off. She liked him for that. He padded into her room, silent in his thick green socks, and stood smiling down at her. Kitty took a deep breath and stepped back from him. Her already small room seemed to shrink to the size of a telephone box.

'Would you like a cup of tea?' she asked him politely, but as she turned away to make it, she wondered if she had made a mistake in inviting him in.

As soon as Kitty stepped back away from him Max remembered his vow not to intimidate her this time. He would start by trying to make himself look small. He folded his long legs with difficulty and sat on one of the low cushions next to the low table. There! Now he took up less room. He put his elbows on the top of the table and looked around him.

He saw that all the furnishings were

Japanese. He rather admired Kitty for living Japanese-style instead of insisting on Western-style lodgings. But then, he already knew that she was the adventurous type.

He couldn't help watching her slender back as she moved over to the tiny gas ring that sat next to the equally small sink unit next to the door and popped the kettle on. She was wearing pink again, some kind of soft pink sweatshirt over comfortable-looking grey leggings, and her auburn curls were swept up on top of her head. Max eyed them closely. It wasn't a very efficient arrangement. Curls tumbled everywhere and he could be mistaken but . . .

'Is that a sock holding up your hair?' he asked curiously as he took the cup of tea that Kitty was offering him.

He admired the lovely pink that coloured her cheeks as she answered defensively.

'I'm house cleaning! I wasn't expecting guests.'

'It looks cute,' he assured her quickly, and more colour stained her cheeks.

He took a sip of tea. The strong smoky flavour rolled over his tongue.

'Nice tea.'

Although she brought her own cup over to the low table and sat down companionably across from him, Kitty ignored the compliment.

'What brings you here?' she asked, taking a sip of her own tea.

Max found himself watching her lips as they pursed over the rim of her fine china cup. They were soft and pink and beautiful. He shook himself and turned his attention to Kitty's question.

'I've come to apologise, really,' he said.

Kitty looked at him with astonishment, and to Max's pleasure, a little admiration, too.

'Well, that's big of you,' she said, nodding those ridiculous curls in satisfaction. 'I like a man who's prepared to admit he's in the wrong occasionally.'

'From first to last, more or less,' Max said sweepingly.

If Kitty would just keep looking at him with those softening blue eyes and that friendly expression, Max Preston was going to apologise even more handsomely than he had first intended.

'I was 'way out of line, barging into your school and interrogating you like that. I'm sorry. Can we start over?' he asked, holding out his hand.

Kitty flashed him an enchanting smile and held out her own hand at once.

'Of course we can,' she said sweetly.

Max took her slim little hand in his own big brown one and examined it curiously. Her hand was tiny. The skin was fine and pale, and each elegant finger was tipped with a pink varnished nail. He examined this hand until Kitty tugged it away from him and even then he let go reluctantly. Kitty smiled up at him cheekily.

'How's the terrorising business going?'

There was a teasing light in her eyes as she spoke. Max felt hot and he moved his long legs, trying to get more comfortable under the low table.

'I don't usually do too much of that,' he protested.

'Then how did you get so expert at it?' Kitty persisted mercilessly.

Max held up his hand.

'I guess I deserve to be teased a little,' he said weakly, 'but I apologised, didn't I? What more can a guy do?'

Kitty seemed to relent. She was examining his wrist.

'I see you got your watch strap mended,' she said.

Max was glad to have the subject changed.

'Yeah, I was real glad to have this watch back,' he admitted. 'My mom gave it me when I graduated high school, just before she died.'

The words seemed to hang in the air. Max was amazed that he had spoken them. He never spoke of the lonely pain inside him. He never told anyone about the rawness that had been his ever since she died. He kept his eyes on his watch and swallowed, wishing he'd kept quiet.

Then he felt Kitty's soft hand touching his. A clean, floral scent drifted towards his nose and he sensed her leaning across the low table to comfort him.

'Max, I'm so sorry,' she said, and that was all, but there was feeling of real comfort and sincerity about her reaction, so much so, that to his great astonishment, Max heard himself add, 'Yeah, it was tough. There was only Mom and me, you see. Dad ran off when I was born and Mom was an orphan.'

And then he felt as if he'd exposed too much of himself. He shook off the soft hand that rested so naturally on his and sat up straight.

'Yes, well, the army is my family now, so let's talk about that.'

His voice sounded gruff even to him and Max faltered to a halt. He was conscious of a deep feeling of gratitude to Kitty when she tactfully followed his lead.

'You tell me you're not in the department of terrorising, so what exactly is it that you do in the army, Mr Preston?'

Max had his cover story ready.

'I'm a combat instructor,' he said, and went on to tell her a few details.

The warmth and interest in Kitty's sparkling blue eyes as he talked made Max feel slightly guilty, but only slightly, because he truly did take a few combat classes. It was just that he did a lot else that he wasn't telling her about. Still it was a rare and seductive pleasure to have a delightful female hanging on one's every word, and Max began to unwind and revel in the situation. He was surprised how warm and comfortable he felt, and how quickly an hour flew by as he sat chatting in Kitty's homey, little apartment.

'What else do you do besides work?' Kitty asked him eventually. 'You seem pretty committed to the job, but even the dullest dog has to take a few hours off.'

Max wrinkled his brow.

'Well, I go jogging pretty much every day.'

Kitty shook her head, and the mischievous sparks that flew from her blue eyes sent tingles down his spine. It was a new and agreeable sensation to be teased in this way.

'If you have to keep fit for your job, running counts as work. What do you do in your real time off? You must leave the base sometime.'

Max was puzzled now, as he thought about his daily routine. What did he do to relax? He flipped through a magazine occasionally, or watched a video with the surveillance team after hours, but his work absorbed him completely. Max realised that he didn't do anything with his life other than work. It seemed a very dull way to live, suddenly.

He looked up, ready to admit as much, and met Kitty's merry blue eyes. She was shaking her head, knowing his answer already.

'You must take some time off!' she scolded him. 'Aren't there any nice restaurants in Yokuska? If you fed your students occasionally, it might give them the strength to survive your combat class.'

'What and make them soft?'

Max laughed, privately thinking that it was a good idea. His students were great kids. He should treat them sometime, and then cold water washed over him. How had Kitty found out where he taught his class? All Max's doubts came flooding back.

'Who did tell you I was stationed in Yokuska?' he barked.

Kitty looked at him with startled, honest eyes. But then her hand came up to cover her mouth and her wide blue eyes dropped away. All Max's training in the art of reading body language told him that she was about to tell him a lie. He felt sick inside.

'Why, no-one, that is, I think you did,' she stammered.

Max felt really angry with himself. He had carried out the first part of his mission and made friends with Kitty, but in the pleasure of talking to a soft and admiring woman, he had forgotten all about the second part of his mission, which was to find out how much she knew. There was no way he would have breached security and told Kitty where he was based, so who had told her? He glared at her fiercely. She'd been softening him up, seducing him away from his mission, and he'd been falling for it.

'I just assumed you were stationed at Yokuska,' Kitty faltered. 'It's the main American naval base, isn't it?'

Her body language was still false. Her hand was still covering her mouth, and even in his distraction Max couldn't help thinking what a shame it was to cover those delicious lips, and her blue eyes were still turned uncomfortably away from his.

'You're lying to me, little lady,' Max said softly.

He was keeping a tight hold on the anger and disappointment that were sweeping over him. The severity of his emotions startled him. Why should he be so surprised and upset because a criminal was lying to him? All criminals lied, he knew that, and he wouldn't be here talking to Kitty if he didn't suspect her of being up to her pretty neck in the weapons smuggling racket.

So why did he feel so bad about it?

Max shook himself all over and fell into his familiar rôle of army interrogator. He hooded his own eyes to mask the surging anger he felt as he spoke.

'I'd really love to know how you found me.'

Kitty's hand fell from her mouth and she looked up at him cautiously, but she didn't actually speak. Max brought into play all the verbal skills that he had learned in order to extract confessions without using force.

'I guess I was a little sceptical earlier when you tried to explain the way it was,' he suggested.

Kitty nodded so vigorously that her curls flew around over that ridiculous sock she had them tied up with.

'Sceptical?' she questioned. 'Downright disbelieving is the way I'd describe it!'

Max was caught by the incongruity of interrogating someone who was using a sock to hold up her cascade of curls, but he was too deeply into his professional mode now to be completely distracted.

'Maybe you could run it by me again,' he suggested.

'I don't know.'

Kitty hesitated. She looked up at him and Max saw caution and wariness in the big blue eyes that met his.

'Well,' he said, casually, almost as if it didn't matter, 'we've been doing so much better second time around. I just thought . . . '

He let the words trail off invitingly as, to his surprise Kitty, began fishing down the front of her sweatshirt. As he watched, puzzled, Kitty withdrew a fine gold chain for his inspection. A crystal tear glittered from the end of it. Max looked at the necklace and then stared at Kitty uncomprehendingly.

'This is my pendulum,' she confided. 'I told you how I used it to find you. I believe in its powers although most folk are just cynical and treat it as a joke.'

Max's jaw dropped open and this time he felt real fury. He'd completely misread her! He'd thought that she was about to tell him the truth, that he'd learn about her sources of information, and instead she was giving him the most ridiculous run around once again! A pendulum! Max snorted. She'd be reading his tea leaves next. He didn't know if he was more angry with her for fooling him or at himself for falling for it, but either way, it was time for him to leave.

Max tried to spring to his feet, but, after more than an hour folded underneath a low Japanese table, his legs had gone to sleep. He stood swaying painfully on his numb limbs and looked down at her. She was twisting the slender gold chain of her pendulum between her fingers. Puzzlement and hurt were clear on her face.

She was a great little actress, Max reflected grimly, either that or whatever sexual enchantment she had been working on him had completely affected his judgement. How did she get those blue eyes to look so innocent and misty? Then a vicious tingling just above his knees made him curse aloud.

'Blast! Pins and needles,' he exploded.

Kitty eyed him cautiously.

'Is that what made you jump up like a scalded cat?'

'No, it is not!' he yelled, feeling driven beyond endurance. 'It's you!'

He broke off and began rubbing his legs vigorously, finding relief in the action.

'Me?' Kitty queried, a dangerous glint beginning to creep into her eyes. 'And what exactly have I done?'

It was a relief to shout, Max was

discovering. Shouting was a wonderful way of relieving the roller coaster ride of emotion he had been on ever since entering Kitty's apartment. In fact, Max realised that he'd been wanting to shout ever since he'd met this distracting British redhead!

'It's what you were about to do!' he snarled, still rubbing his legs feverishly.

'I was about to explain to you about my pendulum,' she said, the sweetness of her tone at distinct odds with the definite battle light that was now shining from her eyes.

'Pendulum be blowed!' Max howled, not even bothering to ask himself why he was losing control so completely. 'Do you think I'm a fool? You already tried that one on me. I didn't buy it then and I'm not buying it now! What made you think you could drag out that shop-worn old story and try it again?'

Kitty's tone was icy.

'Because it just happens to be true,' she said. 'If you have trouble believing that, well, it's your problem, not mine.

Thank you for coming here to shout at me again. I'm sure the whole house enjoyed it, but I'd like you to leave now.'

Max's emotions nearly choked him. He banged at his infuriatingly maddeningly tingling legs and wondered why it didn't make him feel better. He felt guilty now, of course. By reminding him of his promise not to shout at her, Kitty had made him feel like a heel. And Kitty had also reminded him that the whole house would have heard every word. What kind of secret agent was he? He'd failed in his mission again. He was no nearer to finding out what lines of information the gang had and just how Kitty tapped into them. All he could do was beat a dignified retreat.

Max limped as far as the low wall on the other side of the road to Kitty's apartment and sat in the sunshine groaning while he waited for his head to clear and his limbs to work properly again. How had everything gone so horribly wrong? Max went back over the conversation and was certain that he had said nothing aloud about his mission or his true reasons for visiting Kitty, but still, he was deeply grateful that no-one from the team had been around to see the complete hash that he had made of things!

What had happened to the cool, competent professional Max had so carefully trained himself to be? He hadn't behaved so awkwardly since he'd been a gawky teenager, crippled by his first crush!

'Oh, no!' Max said aloud, horrified by the direction his thoughts were taking. 'Oh, no! Oh, no!'

Kitty was just a very skilful operator, that was all. Hadn't his old teacher warned him to be careful with women?

'The female of the species is deadlier than the male,' he always used to say, and now Max could see what the old veteran meant.

But he hadn't fallen for her. Oh, no! She'd nearly gotten under his skin and convinced him that she was innocent, but she'd made a mistake playing that old pendulum card, and although Max had to admit that he hadn't gotten any information from her, at least he was wise to her now.

'She's good though,' he muttered to himself admiringly. 'Very good. So much so that I think I'll stay away from her in future.'

He got to his feet. His legs were fine now as he began to walk to where he'd parked his car. It was a wise man who knew when he was beaten. He would let the Australian operative, John, the ladies' man, have the next crack at Kitty. He was going to stay right away from her. He was never going anywhere near her again.

And that was then he heard the screaming . . .

5

After Max left, Kitty walked around her tiny room spluttering with rage. How dare he, she asked herself furiously. He encouraged me to tell him about my pendulum! He asked me to run it by him again! He said we were getting on so much better!

Kitty picked up her Japanese tea pot and the two tiny matching cups that she and Max had been drinking out of and shoved them vigorously under the tap. They had been getting on so much better, but she'd been a fool to think that they could ever get on for long. How could she, Kitty, with her dreamy nature and strange, psychic ability, ever get on with a man who was as cool, practical and work-orientated as Max Preston?

Kitty banged the now spotlessly clean china on to her tiny draining-board.

She'd been a fool to ever let him in the door, and next time she saw him, she'd tell him so! The glass screens that divided her room from the balcony-terrace were still open. A slightly furtive, scraping noise from outside caught Kitty's attention. She thought of Max's original approach. She could hardly believe that he was daring to come back, but there was definitely a dark shadow approaching. She planted her fists on her hips and swung around to face the open wall. Right! This time she was going to tell him!

Kitty had been so sure that the approaching dark shadow was Max, that, as the figure brushed by the pushed-back screens and turned into her room, it took her a few seconds to realise that this was a complete stranger. He was too small to be Max, much too small, and he moved in a creeping snake-like way that was nothing like Max's firm military tread.

The figure was dressed all in black, a sinister mask obscuring his face. When he saw that Kitty was waiting for him, obviously ready for him, he hesitated for a split-second in the entrance to the room.

Kitty's mouth had been open to spit out a few stinging remarks at Max. Now, instead, she drew in a deep lungful of air and screamed loudly. To her dismay, the dark figure, although it glanced back uneasily, showed no signs of running away. In fact, he took a step towards her, and then another one.

'Max!' Kitty screamed. 'Max! Help me!'

There was no time to wonder why she should be shouting for the man she loathed and had just turned out of her room, but her brain was working as fast as it ever had. The mysterious attacker barred the way out on to the balcony terrace, and there was no time to run to the other side of the room, to the sliding door that opened out on to the corridor. As soon as she turned her back on him, he'd be on her!

Kitty screamed even more loudly at

the thought of being grabbed by the small, but deadly and repellent black figure before her, and she looked around her frantically for a weapon. Her room was so small — and so empty. In keeping with the Japanese custom, Kitty rolled up her bedding, her futon, every morning and put it away in the long cupboard that filled the third corner of the room. There wasn't even a pillow to hit him with, and she hadn't brought any ornaments or pictures here with her. What could she use to defend herself?

She twisted away from the approaching figure, but the room was so tiny it was impossible to run far. She was trapped in a corner. Kitty was aware of her chest heaving as she filled her lungs for another frantic scream. And then she saw it, hanging from the ceiling — the present from her students.

The traditional Japanese cricket festival is marked by the giving of live crickets, and Kitty had received, not only a number of very lively crickets, but also a charming bamboo cage to keep them in. She reached up quickly and pulled the bamboo cage down off the ceiling. She yanked it so quickly and fiercely that the hook the little cage had been swinging from came right out of the beam. Kitty smashed the cage down hard over the intruder's head.

The flimsy bamboo shattered at once and shrilling crickets leaped everywhere. Kitty distinctly saw one fly down the open-necked shirt of her assailant. He gave a yell and reached in after it, but the insect eluded him and he began scratching fiercely. Kitty seized her advantage and stepped back. She picked up the heavy top from her low, Japanese table and briskly whacked the intruder's thighs with it.

Suddenly, the sliding door to the corridor slid open briskly and the landlady, Mrs Ono, stood in the entrance brandishing a sweeping brush. The intruder took one look at her determined face and broke for the open screens. But Max Preston suddenly appeared on the balcony terrace.

There was a fierce scuffle, and Kitty distinctly heard the masked intruder cry out in pain. He vanished and Max came over to her quickly. She could see concern blazing from his eyes.

'Are you hurt?'

'No,' she replied faintly, but her knees were sagging and there was a peculiar singing noise in her ears.

Strong arms took hold, and Max gently forced her to sit down. He made sure that she was comfortable, fetched her a glass of cold water, and then, while Kitty sipped it gratefully, trying to control the nasty waves of shock that were making her so powerless, Max took charge with a completeness and efficiency that left her breathless and admiring.

He dealt with the landlady and Kitty had to admire the way he soothed and charmed her. Max also dealt with the local policeman, who had arrived by bicycle to check out the disturbance. He spoke a little fractured English, but to Kitty's amazement, Max spoke to him in competent, easy-sounding Japanese. The policeman spent a long time examining Kitty's apartment. However, apart from a few stray crickets, he found nothing, and eventually left, shaking his head.

'He's going to ask the neighbours to keep a look-out for suspicious characters,' Max said, coming back across the room to talk to Kitty. 'I've asked Mrs Ono to mention it to the other students, too. I gather there's a couple of Americans who are studying the martial arts staying in the room next to you. That makes me feel better.'

'Why's that?' Kitty asked tartly. 'Because you could send them around to bully me in your absence?'

Max's eyes widened.

'I thought I heard my name shouted earlier,' he said innocently. 'Perhaps I shouldn't have answered.'

Kitty felt her cheeks sting. She had called out for Max instinctively. Something about that embarrassed her very much. She bent her head and took a sip of water. The glass trembled in her hand. Max reached out and gently removed the glass from between her shaking fingers and his tone was surprisingly caring when he spoke.

'Poor Kitten! I shouldn't tease you. You are still suffering from shock. I'm going to make you some hot, sweet tea.'

'Don't bother,' Kitty said faintly, but she had to admit that, as she sipped the strong sweet brew, she began to feel a great deal steadier.

'You've cut yourself,' Max said, gently touching her arm.

Kitty shuddered all over at his touch. That betraying heat stained her cheeks again. To hide it she turned her head and looked at her arm.

'It's only a little scratch,' she said. 'It looks like a scratch from the bamboo bars of the cricket cage. It's nothing.'

Max was already filling a bowl with hot water.

'Do you have any antiseptic? Even the smallest scratch can turn nasty, and

I don't want you dying of a deadly cricket-borne infection.'

She gave him instructions on where to find it, then he carefully poured a few drops from the little bottle into a bowl and carried it over to Kitty. The nostalgic tang of the antiseptic touched her nose as he began dabbing at her arm with gentle, caring movements.

She was very aware of his closeness as he gently tended to her wound. She felt both soothed by his ministrations and unsettled by the intimacy as he continued to bathe her arm. Then his shoulders began to shake with laughter.

'A cage full of crickets! What an unusual weapon!' he said, looking at her with fun-filled eyes. 'You are a very resourceful woman, Kitten Kat Bond!'

Kitty pushed his hand away from her arm.

'Don't call me that,' she snapped. 'And leave my arm alone. I don't need you to do it.'

The merriment left Max's eyes and

he sat back on his heels and looked at her steadily.

'You need someone to look after you. Today could have ended in a lot more than a scratch, you know.'

'I don't need anyone to help me,' Kitty said stubbornly.

'You do,' Max said, equally stubbornly.

Kitty was about to answer him when a cricket jumped out of nowhere and landed on her sweatshirt. She yelped and looked around her. Her apartment was teeming with lively, hopping crickets. She had to catch them. She gave Max a mischievous smile.

'Maybe I do need help,' she conceded.

The beginnings of a faintly smug smile tugged at the corner of Max's lips before he replied.

'Of course, you do,' he said, relaxing a little.

Kitty gave him her best helpless-little-woman smile.

'I'm afraid I might not be able to

cope with the situation,' she confessed.

Max's chest swelled slightly.

'I can deal with it,' he said confidently. 'We could trade information for protection.'

Kitty had no idea what he was talking about, so she simply ignored his comment.

'I'm so glad you feel confident,' she cooed. 'You see I have absolutely no idea how to go about catching crickets.'

'Crickets!' Max yelled. 'What have crickets got to do with anything?'

'They'll have to be caught,' Kitty insisted. 'Mrs Ono will kill me if they escape all over the house.'

Max eyed her uneasily, and Kitty suddenly laughed at him.

'You're afraid of crickets!' she accused.

Max shuffled his feet.

'Not at all,' he protested. 'It's just that I think they will find their own way out eventually.'

Kitty jumped to her feet and gently disentangled the cricket that was still clinging to her sweatshirt. She held the little insect out to Max.

'Just hold this one while I find a jam jar or something to put them in.'

'Uh, I'd rather not,' he confessed.

Kitty smiled up at him.

'A crack in the superman façade,' she remarked thoughtfully. 'I rather like it. It makes you seem less like a plastic action man hero.'

'Plastic!' Max spluttered.

'Iron, then,' Kitty conceded. 'Something smooth and featureless anyway.'

She ignored his still angry splutterings and smiled up at him charmingly.

'Well, if you'll excuse me, it looks as though I'll have to catch my own crickets.'

And with that, she dropped to her hands and knees and began crawling around the floor in search of her lively escapees.

Max eyed the delectable back view afforded him by Kitty's rear and swallowed hard. His thoughts and feelings were in a turmoil. Max swallowed again and tried to tear his eyes away from that enticing little bottom, but he found that he couldn't. Kitty's sweatshirt had rucked up slightly, showing a small amount of her narrow white back. That intimate glimpse of vulnerable naked skin made Max feel tender and protective towards her.

That was the trouble, he reflected mournfully. She made him feel too many things. When he'd been doctoring her cut, he had wanted to cherish and protect her. And when he looked at the tumbling auburn curls that spilled over that ridiculous sock, he wanted to laugh as if he were a child again.

His feelings terrified him. Part of him wanted to believe in her desperately, but despite the Japanese policeman writing the mysterious intruder off as part of an outbreak of cat burglary in the neighbourhood, Max had a sinking feeling that the incident only proved beyond doubt that Kitty was involved in some way with the gang. And if Kitty was a criminal, he, Max Preston, team leader, had no business whatsoever getting mixed up with her.

That was the problem, Max thought despairingly. He should have been thinking about his job and where Kitty fitted into the investigation, but all he could think about was how gorgeous she was and what she was doing to him. He had to get control of himself.

Max took a deep breath. He was going to go to the gym, work out until he collapsed and never think about her again. He drew another deep breath and turned to Kitty. She was scrabbling about in a corner, looking cuter than ever, but Max cleared his throat and barked, 'Kitty, I have to be going now.'

Surprised by his tone, Kitty looked up at him. She was about to tease him about his parade-ground manner when she realised that she was also surprised by how much she was going to miss him. She got slowly to her feet and popped another lively cricket into the jam jar she was carrying. She screwed the lid on carefully, struggling to control herself.

Ever since she had met him, Max Preston had done nothing but bully and shout at her. So why did she feel so lost and vulnerable at the thought of him leaving? Kitty put the jar full of crickets on her low table and moved over to Max.

'I'll take them to the park later,' she told him.

Then she shivered all over. It would be dark, and there would be shadows and rustling leaves in the bushes. A park could hide a multitude of masked assailants. She looked up at Max miserably. He seemed to know how she was feeling.

'Give them some lettuce leaves, or whatever it is that they eat, and take the little critters to the park in the morning, when it's light and there are people about,' he advised her.

'It seems very cowardly,' Kitty said slowly, but she knew that she was going to take his advice.

'You have had a stressful experience today,' Max pointed out.

Kitty met the kindness in his eyes gratefully.

'I'm feeling the effects a bit,' she admitted.

There was something so warm and so comforting about the bulk of the male presence beside her. It was nice to know that he was trained to be more than capable of seeing off any intruders, Kitty thought, but then she reminded herself that the person Max Preston went for usually was her.

So why was he being so kind and gentle now, Kitty wondered, as he touched her face with a gentle hand. It was very confusing. He was acting nothing like the bully she had decided he was as he asked her gently, 'Do you think you'll be all right on your own?'

Kitty dropped her head.

'It seems silly,' she admitted. 'I'm usually fine on my own, only, tonight . . . '

Her words trailed off, and once again

Max seemed to understand her.

'You're afraid that you'll keep thinking about the assailant?' he suggested gently. 'That every tiny noise and movement will sound like him coming back?'

Kitty lifted grateful eyes to meet his kind brown ones.

'Yes,' she admitted.

'There's one way to fix that,' Max said, sounding very confident.

'What is it?' Kitty asked warily, warned by the glint in the depths of his toffee brown eyes.

'This,' Max said softly, and he closed the space between them and just touched Kitty very, very lightly on the lips.

Gentle as the touch was, it sent fire and thrills and tingles racing over the tender skin of Kitty's lips and zinging around her body. The urge to throw herself on to his broad chest and cling to him tightly was almost irresistible. Yet at the same time, she wanted to slap his face and send him packing.

For the long, endless moment that Max's lips were in contact with hers, Kitty was torn between attraction and alarm. Both emotions swept over her so strongly that by the time Max let her go, she was panting as if she had run a race. Her heart was beating loudly in her ears as she met his soft gaze. One of her hands crept up to her mouth and touched it lightly, as if to make sure that her lips were still there. He was smiling at her cheekily.

'It's the only known cure,' he announced, 'and it works every time.'

'Cure?' Kitty echoed shakily.

Max's lips curved in an enchanting smile.

'Gave you something else to think about, didn't I?' he enquired.

Infuriating as it was, Kitty had to admit that he was right. She knew that she would think about nothing else but Max Preston's kiss, and her reaction to it, all night. But she didn't want him to know that.

'What am I going to think about?' she

asked, pretending that she didn't understand.

'My kiss,' Max replied, steam-rollering through her pretence with infuriating male arrogance.

As he turned to leave, Kitty eyed his broad shoulders resentfully. No way was she going to admit the effect that he'd had on her.

'I think I'd rather have had something nice to think about,' she shouted after him. 'But you seem to be intent on supplying me with encounters of the other kind.'

Max's broad back still looked jaunty. He needed taking down a peg or two, Kitty decided.

'Do stop round any time you feel like frightening me to death!' she called after him.

6

Frighten her to death indeed!' Max Preston snorted to his Australian teammate, John. 'She'd have been in for a good sight worse experience if I hadn't been there to save her.'

'Sounds like she had the guy on the run before you got there,' John commented, then he stepped back hastily before the glint in Max's eyes. 'What do you think the intruder was after?' he went on hastily. 'And if it comes to that, who do you think it was? If Kitty is in with the gang, why should the gang send someone after her?'

'A rival gang?' Max suggested. 'It wouldn't be the first time that the police have been given valuable infor-mation by criminals hoping to have their chief rivals locked away.'

John nodded thoughtfully.

'You're right, Max, and I think it

needs looking into. When are you going to see her again?'

'I'm not!'

'Oh, yes, you are,' John said. 'Excuse me for giving orders, boss, but a contact like this could be worth hours of watching by outside surveillance. I know a red herring when I see one. Max, with all due respect, you gotta follow this up. It could take another operative months to get as close to this woman as you have.'

Max shook his head. He didn't want to go anywhere near the little lady again. He was annoyed because he couldn't stop thinking about her. He was annoyed because he couldn't control the whirlpool of emotions that had been bubbling around inside his bewildered heart ever since he'd met her.

'I don't have the experience to handle women,' he protested. 'I've been too long in a male-dominated existence.'

'This is your big chance to get some

experience in that direction,' John pointed out.

Max was about to protest again when a sudden thought hit him. Maybe all these crazy emotions were due to inexperience. Maybe if he were to see Kitty again, he could get these troubling feelings under control, get her out of his system.

'Maybe,' he said thoughtfully, but not entirely convincingly.

'Is she expecting to see you again?' John asked.

Max began to laugh.

'Not unless she was serious about inviting me to drop by anytime I felt like frightening her to death.'

John shook his head firmly.

'Take her out for dinner, mate,' he advised. 'Every woman likes a nice meal.'

'Kitty isn't every woman,' Max returned thoughtfully, 'but I'll see what I can do.'

★　★　★

'Are you going to see him again?' Candy asked, stirring the froth on her cappuccino.

'I don't think so,' Kitty said. 'We're totally incompatible.'

'Then why the big sigh?' Candy asked.

'Because he's gorgeous,' Kitty admitted.

A shudder zipped right through her the way it did every time she remembered his kiss.

'Then why not give him a chance?' Candy enquired.

Kitty shook her head firmly.

'He wears a uniform,' she pointed out. 'How could we possibly be compatible? He's too orderly.'

'They say opposites attract.'

'Opposites may attract in the first place,' Kitty replied gloomily. 'Organised men do seem to fancy me, but it's never long before they start trying to reform me, and I hate that.'

It was painful when anyone tried to change her, Kitty reflected, but it could really hurt if someone she cared for began criticising and saying she wasn't good enough for him. And she sensed that she could end up caring for Max Preston, a lot.

'Do you think he'll call you?' Candy asked.

'No. No, I don't think he'll ring. We didn't exactly part on the best of terms. He didn't look as if he were planning to contact me again.'

Kitty felt her mouth turning down at the corners. She added hastily, 'And anyway, I don't want him to ring me. Not at all.'

Candy didn't look a bit convinced so Kitty hastily changed the subject.

'Isn't it time we left this coffee shop? I don't know about you, but I've got students waiting for me.'

At the end of the evening, as Kitty stepped out on to the street outside the school, she got the feeling that she was being watched. She turned quickly, and she wasn't really surprised when she saw Max Preston lounging in the doorway of a closed shop opposite. She approached him.

'Did you want something? she enquired.

'I've been thinking about frightening experiences I could offer you. Would you like to eat fugu with me?'

If anyone else had offered to take Kitty to a restaurant that served the famous, and fabulously expensive, Japanese blowfish, she would have accepted at once. As it was, Kitty wavered for a moment before shaking her head.

'No, I think I'd rather eat something that was guaranteed fit for human consumption tonight, thank you.'

A dark brow raised mockingly.

'How come? I thought you enjoyed living dangerously. After a long evening at work, I thought you'd be craving a little excitement.'

'Not the sort eating poisonous fish would provide,' Kitty said.

Her unruly heart had started to bump at the sight of his handsome face, but she forced herself to turn away and began walking. Max fell into step beside her.

'Possibly poisonous fish,' he pointed out. 'I trust the chef at the place I'm taking you to. He's never lost a customer yet.'

'There's always a first time.'

'Do you want to die without ever having sampled fugu?'

'Do I want to die because I did sample fugu?' she replied tartly, and then, unable to restrain her curiosity, she asked him, 'Have you eaten it before? What's so special about it?'

'Not much,' Max admitted laughing. 'It doesn't taste of much, but it makes your mouth and lips tingle as you eat it.'

Kitty was tempted, and as she met his melting brown eyes, she knew that he knew it.

'It's late,' she said.

'But you have to eat,' he said reasonably.

The cold autumn air bit into Kitty's cheeks. She looked up into the sky. A big silver moon hung there, a Japanese silver moon. What was the point of being in an incredible country like Japan if you didn't take advantage of it? And she was hungry.

'All right, I'll come.'

Max looked pleased, but he commented, 'That's not the most graciously worded acceptance I've ever received.'

Kitty took his arm and laughed up at him.

'I'm not a prim and proper lady,' she teased.

She felt the arm under hers stiffen and Max's face went tight and very grim.

'I know,' he said seriously. 'That's one of the things I want to talk to you about.'

The serious look was still on his face as they reached the restaurant. Kitty stood back a little as he dealt expertly with the Japanese waiters. Then she let him take her coat and usher her to the best table. She liked the way he took charge, but she also appreciated the fact that he turned to her and asked if she minded him ordering for her.

'Of course not! I can't read a word of the menu!'

Max smiled, picked up the handwritten copy of the menu that lay on their polished wooden table, and asked, 'Can you recognise this Chinese character yet?'

He pointed to an elaborate character.

'Not yet,' Kitty sighed sadly.

'That means sake,' Max explained. 'See, the three little splashes that signify liquid. Show it to the waiter and see what happens.'

The hot, fragrant rice wine was brought to their table in a small china flask. Max carefully poured the wine into Kitty's handleless cup. Kitty watched the dark head bent so gravely over the task, and she felt her heart melt. Stop it, she told herself. How can you like this guy? He's a proven bully. You'll see, he's going to start shouting at you any minute now.

But Max seemed determined to treat

her with the greatest respect, and Kitty found herself liking him more and more as they began chatting.

'I'm kind of puzzled by something,' Max said. 'You teach at an English school, yet you live in the student lodgings.'

'I came to Japan as a student,' Kitty explained. 'I study ikebana, but the course only runs in the mornings, so I was delighted when I found an evening job teaching English.'

'Are you a teacher?'

'I have a teaching certificate because I plan to teach ikebana when I get home.'

'So you're not a proper English teacher?'

'I admit that I'm no expert on the English language, although it's amazing what I've picked up, but I take conversation classes. You don't need special qualifications for that.'

'So you're really a flower arranger?'

Kitty eyed him suspiciously. This was a man whose daily work involved such macho items as guns and tanks. Surely he wouldn't be interested in flowers?

But Max drew her out with questions that showed he was taking a real interest in what she was saying, and Kitty found herself enjoying talking to him about her future plans to open a flower shop.

'So, the Japanese angle is going to be your unique selling point,' he said. 'The factor that makes you different from all the other florists around?'

'That's right,' Kitty said. 'It was a wrench to leave all my family behind, and I was terrified by the size of the bank loan I needed to cover my year here, but I got lucky! I fell into some easy money and I've made enough to pay back the loan already.'

Max scowled horribly at that point. Kitty stopped herself from going on to enthuse about the incredible pay for English teaching. She was talking about herself too much. It was time to change the subject. She hadn't missed the wistful look that came into his eyes when she spoke about her large family. She was curious to know more. Was his life really as bleak and lonely as it seemed?

It seemed that it was. The more she heard about his drab, work-orientated background, the more she felt sorry for him. There seemed to be no room for colour and laughter and fun in his daily routine at all.

'And you never go shopping, ever?' she asked him in awe.

Max shrugged.

'What's to buy?' he asked. 'The army supplies everything I might need.'

'Is that why you're wearing green again?' she asked. 'And here's me thinking it was your favourite colour.'

'Red is my favourite colour,' Max said, staring at her two-piece red suit. 'I bet you just light up the office wearing that.'

Kitty felt heat rise to her cheeks and her knees, even though she was sitting down, went dangerously weak. She turned her head, embarrassed by the admiration that was so plain in his eyes.

'Here's the waiter,' she said hastily. 'At last, I get to try fugu.'

As the waiter put two turquoise plates on the table, Max sat back and watched Kitty exclaiming in pleasure. The raw slices of fugu fish had been arranged in translucent petals on the flat plates, so that each serving looked like a huge chrysanthemum blossom. Max picked up his chopsticks and saluted her.

'Here's to adventure,' he said, and took the first mouthful.

Kitty picked up her own chopsticks and took a morsel of fish. Max was amused, and touched, to see that she had taken the sliver of fish from the very edge of the plate, leaving the beautiful pattern as undisturbed as possible. He watched as Kitty lifted the chopsticks to her quivering pink lips and watched as if hypnotised while they parted gently and the tiny scrap of fish slipped between them.

'It's strange,' she cried, laughing up

at him with excitement and adventure in her eyes. 'I can feel my lips tingling! Max, do they look swollen?'

Kitty pursed up her swollen, bee-stung lips and Max shuddered under the strength of his emotions. She must know what she was doing to him, he thought desperately. Was she at her tricks again, trying to seduce him into forgetting his mission? He mustn't forget that he could be dealing with a criminal here. He reminded himself of her reference to easy money, and a great sadness swept over him.

Taking Kitty for dinner had been a new and totally enchanting experience for him. He had never liked the amount of attention that his size and foreign-ness created wherever he went in Japan, but with Kitty on his arm, Max found he enjoyed heads turning. The most beautiful woman in Tokyo was with him! It was an unexpected and heady pleasure, one that Max had never expected to enjoy.

Yet his suspicions threatened to

destroy his delight in her company. He looked at her sadly. He was not free to concentrate on the charming picture Kitty made in her cheerful red suit as she smiled up at him under her curls. He couldn't help smiling back as she waved a morsel of fish at him, challenging him to test it for her, but he wouldn't allow himself to forget his duty again. He had to get her to talk.

As secret agent Max Preston, he leaned across the table and poured more hot wine into Kitty's cup.

'Drink that,' he said smiling, 'and I'll order another bottle.'

He continued to fill Kitty's cup until she was flushed and smiling. Her eyes glowed with happiness.

'I'm so glad to be alive,' she cried.

'So am I,' Max said, refilling her sake cup and clinking his own empty glass against it in a toast. 'This sure is an incredible world we live in, so incredible, that I'm about ready to believe in your pendulum business. How did you find out you could do it?' Max asked, hoping the wine would blur Kitty's memory of his previous scepticism.

'It was at college,' she began. 'One of the mature students was having a baby, and we tried to find out what sex it was using her wedding ring.'

Max was completely at a loss.

'You must have tried it,' Kitty began, and then she broke off and stared at him.

Her huge blue eyes filled with sympathy and Max couldn't help thinking how beautiful she was as she spoke again.

'No, I don't suppose you ever did. I can't imagine you giggling with a group of friends, let alone dangling a wedding ring on a piece of string over a pregnant woman's stomach.'

Max shook his head. He certainly had never done such a thing.

'Too busy marching around a square or polishing your boots,' Kitty said. 'Rational, maybe, but not nearly as much fun.'

Watching the smile in her eyes and

her gently curving lips, Max Preston had to agree, but he prompted her gently to go on.

'Well, the wedding ring was right! It said she was going to have a boy, and she did!'

Max thought about the latest reliable technology for scanning babies in the womb, but decided not to mention it. Right now it was more important to keep her talking.

'And is that how you got interested in pendulums?'

But he was puzzled. A skilful agent would have changed cover stories the moment they saw it was failing to convince. Why hadn't Kitty switched to a more feasible tale for him by now? Maybe she wasn't an experienced operative. Maybe she had just stumbled into the racket and been tempted by the easy money she had talked about. Max's heart twisted.

Kitty smiled up at him and ran a slim hand through her curls, pushing them up off her lovely brow and grinning at

Max with a smile that was a little tipsy, but so friendly and so confiding that his heart twisted all over again.

'I probably wouldn't have given the pendulum another thought,' she said, 'but my father lost all his slides for his lecture on reservoir design. I told you he worked for the water board, didn't I? Well, he'd been invited to give a talk at an Oxford college, to be televised for the Open University. It was such an honour and we were all so proud of him, and then he lost his slides!'

'So?' Max prompted.

Kitty propped her head on her elbows and smiled up at him mistily. All Max's instincts told him that she was exactly what she appeared to be, a sweet, charming and ever so slightly tipsy English girl. She was innocent.

A professional would never come up with such a crazy story, never, Max thought, and his heart was light as Kitty put one confiding hand on his arm and continued.

'We turned the house upside down

but we couldn't find his slides. I used a little heart pendant that Daddy had given me for my eighteenth birthday and held it over a map of our town.'

Kitty paused for a moment, remembering. Max scrutinised the surprise and awe in her eyes as she relived the moment and he felt a few superstitious prickles travelling down his spine as she lowered her voice to a whisper.

'The pendulum moved in my hand. I was almost frightened, the feeling was so strong. It came to rest above the spot on the map where the canal locks were marked. I couldn't believe that Daddy had dropped his precious slides into the canal, but the canal is only ten minutes away from our house so I cycled over there to have a look.'

'And?'

'And there was one of my father's work mates there in a water board van. I went over to him and told him about the lost slides and he said, 'That's funny! I gave your father a lift home last week.' We looked in the van and

109

sure enough — '

'The missing slides!' Max gasped.

Kitty nodded.

'Scary, isn't it? I don't try it very often. It seems too uncanny to use lightly, but it works every time.'

'I'll get the bill,' Max said hastily, and he knew he was running away.

Far from further exposure to Kitty helping him to become accustomed to the strange feelings that were swirling around inside him, he was more confused than ever. He just couldn't, no, he couldn't believe that a silly, superstitious trick could find lost lecture slides. He just couldn't believe it. Yet looking at her open face and trusting eyes he couldn't believe that she was lying.

So where did that leave him? Max tried to stamp down his feelings as he helped Kitty on with her coat, just as he tried to stamp down his strong desire to plant a little kiss just above the curl that waved so charmingly under Kitty's pink and shell-like ear.

He was a trained, professional operative. He had to control his feelings for her. Kitty was guilty until proven innocent, and as he held open the restaurant door, Max reminded himself that there was still the little matter of Wing Fat Lee. As they emerged into the chilly, but well-lit street, Kitty couldn't resist slipping away from Max's side to swing around a lamp-post.

'It's fun,' she cried. 'Come and join me.'

'You're silly,' Max grumbled.

Kitty skipped over to join him.

'So what?' she asked him laughing. 'Is there any law that says we have to be serious?'

Max didn't respond, so she swung away calling out, 'Oh, be off then, Mister Serious. Go and invade a small country or something equally important. Me, I'm in a good mood and I feel like having fun.'

Max caught up with her and Kitty felt an electric thrill as a big, warm hand slipped into hers.

'I'll see you to the train station,' he insisted.

Kitty looked up at him, smiling.

'I feel like singing,' she teased him.

His expression was serious, but a smile tugged at the corners of his mouth.

'I know some good marching songs,' he offered.

Kitty felt hugely encouraged. If he could laugh at himself maybe they had a chance, and she needed that chance. No matter how often she warned herself that it wasn't sensible to like Max Preston so much, she just couldn't help liking him. She tucked her arm back under his. He certainly needed someone to brighten up his life. Why shouldn't she do it?

As they walked arm in arm down the street and turned into the road that led to the train station, Kitty reviewed the situation in her mind. Now that he believed in her use of the pendulum, there seemed to be no problems between them.

So far, at any rate, he had shown no signs of disapproving of her career. Unlike many of her past lovers, he had not been scornful of her frivolous interest in flowers, in fact he had seemed very respectful of her future business plans.

Kitty shuddered as she remembered the accountant who had suggested that she took remedial maths lessons so that she could get a proper job; and the missionary doctor who had suggested that she train as a leprosy nurse so that she could make herself useful in Africa!

Max, on the other hand, had seemed to accept that while the world needed serious people like him, it needed flowers and fun, too. Maybe they did have a chance. Maybe Max needed her to brighten his life.

Kitty tried to imagine Max's bleak and lonely life — no family, no home, no social life outside the army. Carried away on a wave of sympathy, she decided to do something for him. Max had taken her for a lovely dinner.

Perhaps she could repay him with some home-cooking. Kitty began framing the invitation in her mind just as Max came to a halt outside the station she needed for her train.

'Would you like me to see you home?' he asked.

Kitty smiled up at him.

'In some cities I might have said yes, but I never feel scared on Japanese trains. There's no need.'

An awkward silence fell. Max's face was shadowed despite the bright lights of the hotels that clustered around the station entrance. Although it was late at night, trains pulled in and out of the platforms with noisy frequency. Kitty could hear the station announcements as she searched her mind for the right words to ask Max for dinner. She gazed at his handsome profile and hoped for inspiration.

'Would you like — '

'I think we should — '

They broke off laughing, and somehow seemed to have moved closer together. Kitty was aware of Max watching her mouth. Her heart began thumping deep inside her and she moved a little closer to him.

Max bent his head towards hers very, very slowly, giving her plenty of time to back off, but Kitty found herself swaying towards him. As their lips touched, she heard the sound become deeper, softer, breathless, almost surprised. She nestled into his warm, masculine strength and felt as if she'd come home. His arms closed around her protectively as if he were feeling the same kind of completeness.

Max's soft, loving lips moved over hers with demanding intensity. Kitty pressed her whole body up against him, loving the feeling of his nearness. Max lifted his head and looked dreamily into her eyes. Kitty smiled up at him.

'Holy moly,' she said softly.

Max chuckled softly and drew her closer to him. Kitty drew in his own special scent as she rested her head on his chest. She could feel his heart pounding beneath her cheek, and she was glad that he was reacting, that he found this moment special, too.

She nestled closer to him. He seemed to be retreating rather than advancing, she realised dimly.

She pressed closer to him, trying to tell him through the movements of her body how she felt about him, but Max was strangely still in her arms. She lifted her head to look up at him. His face was expressionless and she couldn't read the distant look in his brown eyes.

'Max?' she questioned softly.

He seemed to shake himself and then tore himself out of her arms. Kitty felt cold, bereft, hurt by his withdrawal.

'I'll be missing my train,' Max said gruffly and he turned away decisively.

Kitty watched his retreating back. Emotion surged through her. He was going! No word of when or if they might meet again. He was leaving her!

'Max, hey, Max,' she shouted after

his departing figure.

The firm military pace slowed and he turned and looked back at her. Careless of anyone who might be passing by, Kitty called out to him, 'How about dinner? Tomorrow night at my place?'

Her heart thumped while he considered this. She'd never asked a man out before, but why should she stand by and let a gorgeous hunk like Max Preston walk out of her life? The rightness of their kiss had given her courage, but her mouth was still dry as she listened to a train rattling by and waited for his reply. He waited for the train to pass.

'All right. What time?' he called.

Kitty's heart felt like a starburst and she shouted joyously, 'Half past seven.'

Max lifted his hand in reply and was gone.

Kitty turned to walk into the train station. As she settled herself into her train she thought of nothing but Max.

She began planning what to buy and cook the next day, given the limitations of her tiny gas ring. Kitty hugged herself joyously. He was coming for dinner tomorrow.

7

At the army base next day, Max Preston was sneaking a look at his watch. Three more hours until he would see Kitty again. He heaved a deep sigh. This meeting he was in was taking for ever and so far it was all boring routine. No-one had anything out of the ordinary to report about the movements of the gang.

Max tilted his chair back and squinted at his watch again. Two hours and fifty-nine minutes to go. He rubbed his tired eyes and wished that the fluorescent lights were not so bright. Under their harsh glare, the operations room looked bare and dingy. It was a horrible place to spend any time in, and he'd been here for hours.

Max was just looking at his watch again when John began his report.

'You know that I've been detailed to

watch Miss Fujiyama's place this week, just in case the gang was using it as the central clearing house we're still looking for. Well, I didn't see any of the gang members we knew visiting it, or any foreigners who might have been likely customers for stolen weapons, but she did have one interesting visitor — a certain Katherine Morland.'

Max's chair went back with a crash and he stared at John with his heart pounding and his mouth dry. Kitty went to Miss Fujiyama's house? He felt sick. The Japanese woman in question had made a good thing out of sleeping her way to the top until she was old enough and experienced enough to operate as she did now.

She was selfish, cold and ruthless. She had committed at least one murder since the team had begun watching her. When they moved in eventually, she was going to go to prison for a long, long time. Max wondered if Kitty had originally gotten involved with the gang for the easy money and then had become corrupted.

'The Tokyo police made discreet enquiries for us,' John continued. 'It seems that for the past few months, Katherine Morland has been visiting Miss Fujiyama's luxurious house every week, usually in the afternoons, we're told, but the times do vary.'

Now Max felt angry, furiously, murderously angry.

I'm on my way to deal with that little lady right now, he thought.

Outside Kitty's apartment, he paused to collect his thoughts. During the journey from the base he had calmed down somewhat, but the anger that still pulsed through his veins surprised him by its continuing depth and ferocity.

Max had thought he was immune to such personal feelings. Dealing with criminals as he did, he knew that if he allowed himself to get angry he wouldn't be able to stay calm enough to do his job. Max Preston didn't go in for personal vendettas. He took a detached interest in the criminals he hunted down. Or at least he had, up until now.

Max paced up and down the street outside Kitty's lodgings, battling with his feelings. Why was Kitty so different? He had suspected from the very first moment that she was involved with the gang.

She had made no effort to hide the pleasure she had found in the easy money she said she had made in Japan. Yet Max had wanted to believe her innocent, had begun to believe that she was innocent, still wanted to believe that she was innocent.

He took another turn up and down the narrow street. He had to control his feelings. He was a professional and it was his duty to stay cool and in charge. This time, he was determined to get the truth out of Kitty, but he was also determined to keep his head and judge fairly.

He took a deep breath and entered the student lodgings. There was no-one around as he unlaced his boots and padded towards Kitty's room. Delicious cooking smells wafted through her slightly open door. Entirely forgetting that he was over an hour early, Max stuck his head eagerly through the gap. Then he forgot all about food. There in front of him, bending down, just barely covered by a white fluffy towel, was Kitty.

He must have made some slight sound, because she whirled around and almost screamed out loud before she recognised Max.

'Oh! You gave me a fright! I might have guessed it would be you again.'

She clutched her slipping towel and glanced over at her clock, before looking back at him with indignant eyes.

'You are over an hour early, and don't they teach you how to knock on doors in the army?'

Max knew he should apologise, but he was too entranced by the picture she made. Her wet hair was piled up on top of her head and held back by a towelling bandanna. Her skin was flushed a delicious rosy pink and it still glowed damply from her shower.

Max seemed to be taking her all in at once, and he knew that the details would stay with him for ever.

He was mesmerised by the way her bare toes with their shell-pink nails had curled up in embarrassment.

She looked so gorgeous that it created a tight pain around his heart. He wanted to lift her into his arms and never let her go. Never let her go? What was he saying? Forever meant marriage and commitment. He wasn't a forever kind of guy.

Max swallowed hard. His feelings were in a turmoil. Why was he letting her get to him like this? He still didn't know what to say, so he stood there staring at her.

'Is anything wrong, Max?' Kitty asked, concern in her eyes as she took a step towards him.

He caught a delicious whiff of soap and clean skin. It unnerved him completely. He couldn't bear to feel so vulnerable, so out of control, and with a woman who might be a criminal. His voice was gruff with all his suppressed emotions as he spoke.

'What is your connection with Miss Fujiyama?' he blurted out.

Kitty stared up at him, bewilderment clouding her trusting face.

'Miss Fujiyama? Noriko? She's one of my English students. Max, I don't understand this.'

Confusion threatened to overwhelm Max. Damn her! Every time he tried to pin her down she came up with some answer to confuse him. It was just barely possible that Kitty did teach the woman English, but only just possible. He had to know the truth.

'Where did you meet her? How long has this been going on?'

Kitty's little figure became strangely dignified for a half-naked woman who was wearing only a towel. Her eyes glowed angrily.

'Max Preston, you must stop treating me like an enemy suspect and tell me what all these questions are about.'

Max was taken aback by the fine, hot little temper that met his question. He wasn't used to being confronted. He had been the team leader for many years now, and he was used to people doing as he told them. He knew that he was considered an easy-going, democratic leader, but he also knew that the few times he had blown up were legend. He was famous for the ferocity of his reprimands. Nobody challenged him because they knew what the consequences would be.

Relief washed over him as he realised the problem here. He simply hadn't made it clear to Kitty who was boss around here. All he had to do was bark at her. There wasn't a man on the base who could stand up to that. He crossed his arms over his chest and stared down his nose at Kitty.

'This is a serious business, Katherine Morland. It's time for you to stop prevaricating and tell me the truth.'

'About what, exactly?' she replied sweetly.

Max was relieved by her docile tone. He should have thought of this sooner. Women liked a man to be the boss!

'You tell me everything about your connections with the Lucky Dragon Club, Wing Fat Lee and Miss Fujiyama. Every detail!' he commanded. 'Come along! Start now!'

Kitty looked up at him sweetly. Her lips were curved in an entrancing smile. Looking at them, Max missed the battle light in her eyes.

'Start now, the man says! Now, where would be a good place to start?' she mused, as if to herself. 'Yes, I know. The best place to start would be by telling you to get out of my room and never to come near me again.'

Max felt his jaw drop.

'But — '

'But nothing!' Kitty spat back. 'How dare you march in here and begin interrogating me like that? Max, I don't know what all this secret spy nonsense is about but I'm not explaining myself any more. I'm me, Kitty, just as I am. You have to trust me, Max. Trust me or get out.'

Max cleared his throat. Kitty was nothing like the men he worked with, he was just discovering that, but he had no idea what to do about it. He was baffled.

Even as he barked out his next command, he had a feeling that it wouldn't work.

'I demand that you tell me.'

The beautiful pink lips that he was staring at quivered.

'Then I demand that you get out.'

Judging by the resolution in the blue eyes that met his so firmly, Max knew that she meant it. No amount of bluster or barking would move her. None of his military training had prepared him for a situation like this. He was at a complete loss.

★ ★ ★

'So what did you do?' John asked sympathetically as Max told him to sit down.

Max poured the last of his beer from the bottle into the glass.

'I left,' he said gloomily. 'I didn't want to go back to the base, so I came here. I knew it was your favourite bar and I was hoping to catch you.'

'Why?'

'Because you know about women, John. Tell me what I should do.'

'Marry her, probably.'

'What? I thought you believed in loving them and leaving them. I thought you'd tell me how to get her out of my system.'

John shook his head.

'No can do, mate. The secret is to keep them out of your system. Once a woman gets under a fella's skin, it's too late. It's wedding bells next. Seen it time and time again.'

Max clenched his fists.

'What about Wing Fat Lee?'

'What about him? I wouldn't like my

past held against me.'

'You're advising me to brush aside the fact that the woman I love is mixed up with a criminal gang?'

'Maybe mixed up with a criminal gang,' John pointed out calmly. 'You have no real proof.' He drained his beer and slid off his bar stool. 'Gotta go, Max. There's a nice little lady waiting for me. Don't take it too hard, mate. I'll be your best man.'

'But, John, she's a criminal! It's our job to catch criminals, not marry them.'

'Maybe a criminal,' John pointed out again. 'You wouldn't feel like this if she was really dodgy, Max. Trust your heart, trust Kitty's heart, and if she has fallen into bad company, well, you'll just have to reform her.'

Max ordered another bottle of beer and sat drinking it gloomily. Who would have thought that John with his bachelor ways and never-ending string of girls would have told him to trust his heart and marry Kitty?

Marry Kitty! That was the last thing

he wanted. No, he decided, it was the only thing he wanted! Max heaved a big sigh and propped his chin on his fists.

'The woman I love.'

The words had popped into his head and surprised him, but he knew they were true. There was more to life than love though. There was his career to think about. Max thought he would probably be sent to Antarctica to count snowflakes if his superiors were to catch him marrying an associate of Wing Fat Lee.

And what if Kitty went wrong again? She had seemed so pleased with her easy money. From his studies of criminals, Max knew that very few ever turned away from crime once they had tasted the easy life. It was no good. He had better not think of her. He had better put her right out of his mind, for ever this time.

★ ★ ★

Kitty had pulled her futon out of the cupboard and made up her bed, but she was too miserable to get into it. Wrapped in a clean cotton kimono, she lay on top of the crisp white covers and sniffed miserably. The evening was ruined and a heavy, leaden feeling around her heart told her that her intuition had been right — she had grown to like Max Preston a lot, and it hurt terribly that he disapproved of her so strongly.

She looked around her little room miserably. It looked nice in the soft glow of a pink lamp, and she had automatically tidied away the remains of the spurned dinner, but even the thrill of sleeping in her real Japanese room had no power to cheer her this evening.

'I'm just plain miserable, that's what it is,' Kitty said to herself and she heaved a big sigh.

Perhaps she should write a letter to her family. It seemed all wrong to be lying here doing nothing. Kitty sighed again. She was too miserable to settle to anything.

'Damn Max Preston,' she said, and almost as if the thought had conjured him up, there was a ferocious pounding at her door.

'Come in, Max,' Kitty said, even before she opened the door.

Max barged into her little room and stood glaring at her with angry brown eyes.

'How did you know it was me?' he snarled.

Kitty repressed a smile as she met his furious gaze. Throwing his weight around and blustering he might be, but Max Preston was clutching the biggest bunch of flowers she had seen in a month of Sundays, and, as a florist, Kitty had seen a few!

'I just guessed,' she said sweetly. 'Is there something you want to say to me, Max?'

'Kitty, I can't go on like this.'

Max stopped and stared at her miserably. He had forgotten that he was still holding the flowers and his lovely brown eyes met Kitty's over a froth of blossom.

'I can't stop thinking about you, Kitty! And it's driving me crazy to think that you might be lying to me.'

Kitty's heart melted at the pain and honesty she saw shining now in Max's eyes. She crossed the few steps between them and gently took the flowers.

'Thank you, Max.'

She meant for his openness as much as for the beautiful bouquet.

'I think a lot about you, too, Max, and it's driving me crazy to think that you don't believe in me.'

Somehow, the space between them had shrunk to the width of a fresh-smelling bouquet of flowers. Kitty laid the colourful bunch gently on the floor, and when she straightened up, Max was holding out his arms. She flew into them with a little sound of happiness.

It felt so good to be within the circle of his strong arms once more. It felt so right when his lips touched on hers but

Kitty drew back. Max made a little sound of protest and reached for her, but Kitty put the palm of her hand on his chest. She could feel his heart beating a fast tattoo.

'Let's settle this, Max,' she said.

'I guess you're right. We should fix things between us first.'

He bent his dark head and planted a row of sweet, arousing kisses along her neck just under the chin. Kitty felt her knees quiver with longing, and heat burned along her cheekbones. With a great effort of will, she managed to push Max away.

'The way I see it,' she began slowly, 'the very first argument we had was because you didn't believe that I had tracked you to the military base by using my pendulum.'

'That's right,' he admitted.

Kitty saw his brown eyes clear and sharpen as he began to turn his mind to work. He drew her down to sit beside him on the low cushions next to the table.

'I was assigned to check out how you could have gotten access to military information.'

'Talking about lying, since when has checking out possible spies been part of a combat instructor's job?' Kitty asked looking up at Max indignantly.

Those lovely thick lashes swept down to veil his eyes for a moment, before he looked into her eyes.

'Ah, I was going to tell you about that,' he said.

'Later.'

Kitty put her hand on his arm.

'I deal in flowers. I don't need to know any military secrets. All that matters for now is that we learn to trust each other. Max, if I could prove to you that my pendulum works, would you believe in me then?'

It was hard to read the expression in his eyes, but his voice was confident as he replied, 'Sure, but how are you gonna do that?'

Kitty wrinkled her brow.

'Have you lost anything, or is there

anything you really want to know?'

Max sat bolt upright.

'Sure!'

He reached for the jacket that he'd dropped on the floor as he came in and dug a photograph out of his pocket. His hand shook slightly as he passed the print to Kitty.

'I recognise Miss Fujiyama, but who is the man with her?' she asked, looking down at the picture of a middle-aged oriental man in evening dress. 'Is he lost?'

Max's lips landed noisily on her cheek with a loud, smacking kiss.

'I'm really glad you don't know who that is, because you're looking at a picture of the notorious Wing Fat Lee.'

Kitty turned to Max, laughing.

'He's real! But, Max, I made him up! Or I thought I did. No wonder you suspected me if there really is a Wing Fat Lee. It's too ridiculous a name to be a coincidence.'

Max's arm snaked around her waist.

'You went to the Lucky Dragon Club

and he owns it. Maybe you heard his name then, or saw it written somewhere. It doesn't matter now. But what I would like to know is, where else can he be found? I shouldn't tell you much, Kitty, but I'm close to nailing this guy. All I need is a little more hard evidence that will stand up in court. I think he has a kind of headquarters tucked away somewhere. Find that for me, Kitty, and I'll believe in you for ever.'

Kitty felt a burst of happiness around her heart. She couldn't resist snuggling up and kissing the adorable dimple in the cleft of Max's chin.

'You already do trust me.' She laughed. 'Otherwise you wouldn't have told me so much.'

Max's hard lips came down over hers, and she was breathless by the time she managed to push him away.

'Wait! I've got a street map of Tokyo somewhere. Let me get it.'

★ ★ ★

138

Half an hour later, she sat back on her heels and stared at Max in frustration.

'Why won't you even consider it?' she asked angrily.

Her voice was unsteady and there was a trace of tears in it. Max kissed her lovingly.

'Kitty, I appreciate that you're trying to help me, but, it's just a sushi restaurant you've landed on. How many million sushi bars are there in Japan? It's like ants at a picnic. I don't have the resources to check out a random guess.'

'It's not random. My pendulum — '

'I can't assign an operative to the restaurant unless I can find a concrete link between this restaurant and the gang. This isn't a comic book. I have to fill out forms, Kitty, and explain all my decisions to committees.'

Kitty tried to imagine walking into a room full of men dressed in official uniforms and explaining that she wanted to spend army money based on a tip from a pendulum. Her arms slid around Max's waist and she rested her head on his shoulder.

'Oh, Max,' she said softly, 'I do see what you mean. But we'll have to devise another test for the pendulum. I want you to believe me.'

Max lifted her chin with gentle fingers and began to plant soft, loving kisses along her lips.

'I believe in you, all right,' he murmured. 'Oh, Kitty, I believe in you.'

And this time, Kitty made no attempt to push him away as his kisses became more insistent, more demanding. In fact she melted into his passionate embraces with an eager confidence that she had never known before, kissing him avidly.

Then suddenly, the floor of her room jerked violently. She felt Max's arms close protectively around her.

'Earthquake!' he murmured. 'Hold tight!'

The sickening motion stopped almost at once, but a cacophony of alarms filled the air outside the building. Max put his lips to Kitty's ear.

'That was a sharp one. The vibration from the tremor has set off all the car alarms.'

He held her tighter and kissed the tip of her nose.

'What's so funny?' he asked as she began to laugh.

'Oh, Max,' she giggled. 'The earth really did move for us!'

She felt as much as heard the rumble of laughter that was Max's reaction. Laughter was still smiling out from his loving brown eyes as he bent his head to kiss her once more, and Kitty realised that no amount of common-sense and talking to was going to do her any good. She was completely, totally and utterly in love with Max Preston.

* * *

Next day, she had to attend her flower arranging class in the morning, so Max had decided to come to her flat and prepare a meal for them, unknown to Kitty!

Kitty was full of eager anticipation that afternoon as she hurried home along the street that led from the train station to her flat. She and Max hadn't actually made a firm arrangement to see one another again.

You mustn't be too disappointed if he doesn't appear today, she told herself, but her heart was thudding nervously as she took off her shoes in the entrance to the building and her hand shook as she opened the door.

A huge smile lifted the corners of her mouth as she saw Max's big, muscled body filling her tiny room, but then he swung around to face her and she saw the fury in his face.

8

Max closed the space between them in two quick strides and gripped her by the shoulders. His mouth was a tight line and real anger gleamed in his eyes.

'You went to that blasted sushi restaurant, didn't you?'

Kitty's astonishment was clear in her tone.

'Why, yes, I wanted to check it out for you. But how did you know?'

Max fairly spat the words out.

'Never mind how I knew! You had absolutely no right to put yourself at risk like that.'

Now Kitty felt a confusion of emotions tightening around her chest. She met his furious brown eyes bravely.

'Max, I thought you didn't believe in my pendulum.'

He was so angry that he gripped her shoulders even more tightly and actually shook her.

'I don't!'

'Then why shouldn't I go to the restaurant? It was only for lunch? I thought I could snoop around, see if there was any connection with the gang that I could uncover, then you would have to believe in my crystal.'

'And if there was a connection you could have been killed! How could you be such a fool, Kitty? If the gang had based their headquarters there and you had stumbled right into the middle of an arms deal, they could have killed you. You have absolutely no idea what kind of people you are messing about with.'

'Messing with?' Kitty repeated, feeling a nasty cold pain around her heart.

She looked up into Max's angry face. There was a little muscle jumping next to the corner of his mouth. She fixed her eyes on it.

'I wasn't messing,' she said. 'I found out something important, Max. A Mr Fujiyama owns the restaurant, and he's got a sister called Noriko, just like my student. Is that messing?'

Max shook her again. She wondered how she could have ever found that tense male face attractive as he shouted.

'Yes, messing! This is a gang of ruthless killers. Leave it to the professionals, Kitty. Don't go playing around with things you don't understand.'

The sharp pain in Kitty's chest was getting stronger. A spreading cold feeling drifted over her as she looked up into Max's angry brown eyes.

'Messing,' she said softly, 'playing. Those words tell me what you think of me and my way of going about things, Max.'

Tears suddenly blurred her vision. Kitty knew now that they had no future together. Just like all her other boyfriends, Max had measured her up and found her wanting. True, as yet he had made no attempts to reform her, but it wouldn't be long before he did, Kitty thought sadly. It's over.

She put her own hands under Max's

and pushed them off her shoulders. Max let her go at once and dropped his hands to his sides. Kitty saw they were clenched, but she didn't feel afraid of him. She knew Max would never hurt her, not physically. Emotionally was another matter.

There was a leaden inevitability about the way she felt now. What a fool she had been to think that she could have brought some fun and sunshine into his life. He had been humouring her, allowing himself to be amused, but when it came to a serious matter, just look how he reacted.

Kitty swallowed hard and wished she had never laid eyes on him. She had thought that she had been hurt in the past, but the raging, tearing pain that threatened to engulf her now was so deep, so savage, that she didn't know how to bear it. The only thing she had left now was pride. Automatically, she lifted her chin and went on the attack.

'I still don't understand how you knew where I had lunch today.'

Max had the grace to look slightly embarrassed.

'One of our operatives . . . '

Now Kitty felt an anger beginning to build. Anger was much easier to feel than pain. Kitty allowed the warming, releasing emotion to flow through her as she asked carefully, 'You asked one of your operatives to follow me? May I ask why?'

Colour stained Max's cheekbones but he met her furious gaze calmly and resolutely.

'When I reported in at the base I realised how far I could have compromised security by telling you so much. What if a war broke out because Wing Fat Lee sold a dictator weapons and I didn't stop him? I had no right to put my personal feelings before the success of the operation.'

'So you had me followed?'

'So I had you followed.'

Kitty's feelings were in such a turmoil that she could hardly think straight, but she protested.

'You're not making sense. First you're having me followed as if I were a criminal, next you're storming at me for trying to catch them.'

The spark came back into Max's eyes.

'If I'm not making sense it's because you have turned my whole life upside down, but one thing I do know, and that is that no woman of mine is putting herself into danger while I'm around.'

Kitty faced him angrily.

'But you weren't around,' she pointed out sweetly. 'And whatever you may think of me, Max, and you have made it pretty clear how pathetic you think I am, I want you to know that this is my life and I happen to believe in my way of doing things.'

She choked to a stop. A big lump of emotion gripped her throat like a fist. Max's eyes were dark with emotion.

'Kitty, you don't know what it did to me thinking you might be in danger. You don't know what you're doing! You

148

have to let me keep you safe.'

'Criticism again,' Kitty said, turning her head away.

'What do you mean? I thought women wanted to be protected.'

'Not if it means telling me I don't know what I'm doing.'

'But you don't!'

Kitty exploded.

'Get out!' she yelled at him. 'Get out of here and don't ever come back! You're probably right! I probably don't know what I'm doing. Why else would I let you bully and insult me?'

She dashed angry tears from her eyes.

'But I've learned a lesson from you, Max, and I've made my decision. I'm not going to change, because I like the way I am, but I'll never again spend time with a man who thinks that I'm playing at life.'

Max met her eyes as if he wanted to say more, but Kitty made it obvious that she wanted him to leave and he walked reluctantly to the door, leaving

Kitty to fling herself into a miserable heap in the corner of her room and give way to tears.

But grief-stricken as she was, she knew she was right to break things off with Max now. There could be nothing but misery in life, married to a man who thought that her way of going about things was messy.

She just doesn't understand, Max fumed to himself as he paced round and round the tiny park a few blocks from Kitty's apartment. She just doesn't understand how dangerous these criminals are.

What if she did understand, an inconvenient voice deep within his mind asked. What if she understood the danger but disregarded it because she wanted to help you?

Max tossed the thought out of his mind and strode past a grove of brilliantly red Japanese maples without noticing them. She'd thrown him out! But then he realised that Kitty wasn't one of his men. What right had he to bawl her out? Max was starting to feel rather uncomfortable. A little voice was forcing him to face some unpalatable truths.

I've gotten too used to bossing people about, Max thought regretfully. I've handled Kitty wrongly all along.

He had reached another clump of beautiful red maple trees. He came to a stop in front of them and regarded their glorious autumn colours absently while he struggled to straighten out the tangle of emotions in his mind. One thing was very clear. Whatever he felt about Kitty putting herself into danger, he had no right to shout at her like that.

I still feel that my assessment of the situation was right, he thought, but I shouldn't have gotten angry, and I shouldn't have put her down. No wonder she got mad at me!

Max began walking again, more slowly this time, feeling the gravel crunch under his feet. He felt real admiration for Kitty. She was true steel. He knew how hard he could be to stand up to, but she hadn't wavered an inch. She had gotten upset, and no wonder, but she had steadfastly held by her values and judgements. He loved her for that.

Max swung around with decision and walked briskly out of the park. Pendulums and scattiness, none of it mattered a scrap. He couldn't approve of Kitty's way of going about things, of course, but he loved her. He would go back and tell her so, and woo her, and who knows, maybe marriage would steady her.

Just before Max reached Kitty's lodgings, he heard a confused shouting. He broke into a fast run. Was that a gunshot he heard? Max quickened his pace to an all-out effort, but he still only arrived in time to see the tail-end of a long, black limo as it cruised out of the narrow street.

Mrs Ono burst out of the door of the building brandishing her sweeping brush. Max ran up to her.

'Not Kitty!' he yelled.

Mrs Ono nodded vigorously.

'Bad men took her. Look like gangsters to me.'

Max took a few steps in the same direction that the limo had taken but pulled himself up sharply. Ridiculous to chase a car on foot. He swung on his heel and ran. Thank goodness he had driven into town today. There was a radio in the car as well as a mobile phone. He could call the base and have them . . . Have them what?

The answer to his question came just as he reached his car — order a raid, rescue Kitty. His hands shook as he dialled the number that would connect him with the team back at the base. As he reported the latest events, his thoughts moved swiftly. His only priority was getting Kitty back. But it wasn't that simple. The only reason his team hadn't moved in on the gang was because they didn't have quite enough information to nail them. And that lack of information could mean Kitty's death.

All Max's training and intuition told him that the gang would have taken her to their headquarters, the one place his team hadn't been able to locate yet. A crackling voice drew his attention back to the handset.

'If you think the time is right, that's good enough for the top brass. We're officially cleared to mount a raid, Max.'

A little of the tension left his shoulders. He would have gone against his superiors if necessary, but they hadn't questioned his judgement, this time. Max knew that this raid would spook the gang. If the raid didn't get the information as well as Kitty, the operation would be over, and with it his whole career. He pushed the thought out of his mind. It didn't matter now. Nothing mattered but Kitty.

'We'll be ready to go in about ten minutes, Max,' the distant voice continued. 'What location did you have in mind as a rendezvous point?'

Max's heart beat so fast it threatened to knock him off his feet. He sagged limply against his car. Think! Think, he told himself over the desperate roaring that filled his ears.

In his mind's eye he saw the limousine taking off with squealing tyres in the direction of the freeway. Impossible to tell which way it would turn when it got there. Are you crazy, his mind questioned. They'll be going to the Lucky Dragon Club! Where else would they go?

But in the time they'd watched the Lucky Dragon Club the team never saw the masterminds entering or leaving. They operated somewhere else, I'm sure of it, Max decided.

The masterminds were Wing Fat Lee and Miss Fujiyama, clearly. Could it be her house they used? We had it watched and Kitty was the only person who went there, he was thinking.

Oh, Kitty! Max's heart tore inside him and he wished violently for his time with her back again. Images of her filled his mind. Her auburn curls tumbling over that ridiculous sock; her nestling into his arms and laughing at earth-quakes; looking at him so sadly.

'I'm me, Kitty, just as I am. You have to trust me, Max.'

Her remembered voice chimed softly in his ears and he would have given anything to step back in time and sweep her up in his arms and cry, 'I do trust you, I do.'

The voice haunting his memories was drowned by the crackling of the real voice on the radio.

'Say again, Max. I don't get the location.'

Max pushed his fists urgently against his forehead. If he got this wrong, he'd never see Kitty alive again. He thought of her kneeling so seriously over the Tokyo map, twirling her crystal over the sushi restaurant, while he admired her darling pink lips and serious expression.

Kitty's pendulum! Could he trust it? He was a soldier. He dealt in facts, hard data. He moved from concrete plans to real location. He didn't operate on hot air and moonshine and pendulums.

A Mr Fujiyama owned the restaurant, and he had a sister called Noriko, Kitty had said. There were two hard facts. Max groaned when he thought of the stakes. The whole team had worked so hard on his operation, and he knew that more than one promotion depended on its success. There was international prestige to consider. How the world's Press would laugh at America if her team leader made the wrong move now.

And as for his career — if he made the wrong decision, he would be thrown out of the army. He might even be court martialled for allowing a woman to affect his judgement.

None of it mattered alongside Kitty. For Kitty's sake, he had to make the right decision, and make it fast. Max Preston lifted the radio.

'OK, team,' he said, and the calmness of his tone gave no indication of the turmoil inside him. 'This is what we're gonna do.'

9

Kitty stared into the calm face of the elderly oriental man with sharklike eyes who sat facing her across the polished desk.

'Wing Fat Lee,' she said, and it wasn't a question.

He bowed his head.

'Very wise of you not to pretend to be the outraged innocent. Hand it over.'

There was a powerful air of menace underlying Wing Fat Lee's calm and almost genial manner. He was not a man to antagonise with direct refusals. Kitty's mind raced. Hand over what? What was she supposed to have? Information about Max's operation? Perhaps if she could get him talking all would become clear.

'And if I don't?' she asked.

Wing Fat Lee shrugged.

'I hardly like to think of a charming

young lady like yourself finding out.'

That made the stakes clear. Funnily enough, Kitty couldn't summon up the energy to worry about her own safety. She was so miserable about losing Max that being kidnapped and threatened hardly added to her misery at all.

'What happens if I give it to you?' she enquired now.

'You get to go home and live a long and happy life.'

Again, clear enough, or it would be if only she knew what it was she was supposed to have. Kitty tried a cautious probe.

'Could you just clarify exactly what you expect from me and exactly what I get in return?'

Wing Fat Lee shifted impatiently on his chair.

'You are hardly in a position to ask questions,' he pointed out, 'but if it will hurry things along, you tell me where you have hidden the missile piece you stole from the Lucky Dragon Club. You stay here while my operatives fetch it.

Once I am satisfied that I have the correct item, in good condition, I shall release you.'

'Really?' Kitty asked sceptically. 'Even though I've seen your face and know where your headquarters are?'

'Really. I am not a monster, Miss Morland. I will, of course, have you escorted out of Japan. You cannot be allowed to contact any of the authorities in this country, but you will be safe enough at home. You have my word.'

'What if I go to the police back home?'

'You are going to promise me that you will not, and in any case, I don't think you will find that the British are terribly interested in what happens overseas.'

Kitty supposed she should be glad that she wasn't going to be murdered. And then she remembered that she was only going to get home if she gave Wing Fat Lee the weapon component he was after. She might be horribly murdered after all!

'This, er, weapon,' she began cautiously, 'could you just describe it to me? I'd hate to make any mistake over this.'

'The mistake was in you ever getting your hands on it at all! My client was furious when he found that the cyber disc was missing from his missile. My only concern is that I will be his next victim if I don't return the missing unit. Come along, Miss Morland, I'm growing tired of this interview. Where do you have the disc hidden?'

Wing Fat Lee shifted impatiently. Her thoughts had been working overtime and she was now clear as to exactly what this evil man was seeking.

She found it hard to believe that the pretty golden dish under her maple tree bonsai could be so important.

'Why didn't you just steal it back from me?' she asked him.

'Because you've hidden it. I had your room searched. I know it isn't there.'

Then you know nothing, Kitty said to herself, and knowing that the gang could make mistakes gave her hope.

She decided to play for time, ignoring the dangers. She had what they wanted and would do nothing to harm her until it was safely back in their hands.

Wing Fat Lee rapped sharply on his desk.

'Where is it, Miss Morland? Do not waste my time!'

What could she tell him? Where could she send them that would buy her some time? The school where she taught English? Too close, and she couldn't risk her students getting hurt. The coffee shop by the school? Too close again. She needed to send them far away.

Then Kitty had it — the perfect place! The restaurant where she'd had dinner with her students, the night Mr Tanaka had left his wallet and so precipitated the chain of events that had ended up here, with Kitty facing Wing Fat Lee in his office over a sushi restaurant in downtown Tokyo! She took a shaky breath and told him where the restaurant was.

'There's a bookshelf full of old books at the back of the room,' she told him. 'No-one ever uses it. I hid your disc behind the books.'

There was a serious warning in Wing Fat Lee's even tones.

'It had better still be there.'

'I'm sure it will be,' Kitty said.

As she was led from the room by two silent and unsmiling gangsters, her mind was working furiously. How long had she got? Where were they going to put her, and how could she escape?

Her prison turned out to be a room at the end of a long corridor. Left alone, Kitty paced the empty room and thought that it might have been expressly designed as a prison.

For a start, it was completely empty. No handy sheets to use as ropes; no chairs to stand on; nothing she could use as a weapon or to break her way out. The bare floor was entirely covered in soft tatami matting. There was nothing on it at all.

The door and walls were made of metal, and the small, metal-framed windows were locked. They were too small to crawl out of, even if she could have smashed the tiny panes of wired security glass with her bare hands, which she couldn't.

Kitty's heart began to beat more rapidly as she took yet another turn around the room.

Max, maybe Max will save me, she thought. Don't be a fool, she chided herself. Even if Max came looking for her, he wouldn't come here because he thinks the pendulum is no more than a plaything. He didn't believe the crystal when it located the gang at Mr Fujiyama's sushi restaurant. She couldn't rely on Max to get her out of this.

She looked up at the ceiling. She knew that Japanese buildings were not as solid as their British counterparts. In the past, light buildings of bamboo and paper were preferred because they did far less damage if they collapsed in

Japan's frequent earthquakes. Even in modern times, the tradition of light construction remained. If she could get up into the roof space, maybe she could claw her way out.

Twenty minutes later, Kitty fell back on the tatami matting, sweating and gasping. The ceiling was far too high for her even to jump up and touch with her fingertips, and there was no way she could scale the smooth metal walls.

She laid her head on the soft rice-straw matting. How long did she have left? How long before the gang got to that restaurant and discovered she'd lied to them?

If Wing Fat Lee hadn't gone with them, she had only half the time she'd originally estimated. He could be waiting here, and his henchmen could phone him.

Kitty gave a soft groan and pressed her cheek into the tatami matting. The hay-like scent met her nostrils. She'd loved the scent of tatami ever since arriving in Japan. Now it might be the last thing she ever smelled.

Kitty's mind wandered. She'd been so pleased when Mrs Ono had replaced the worn piece of the mat by the door of her room. The new piece smelled strongly of fresh hay, and it was a darker, greener colour than the other rectangles of matting in her room. The rice-straw turned golden with age and the scent faded.

Kitty sat bolt upright. Tatami matting was supplied in rectangular blocks! It could be lifted and replaced. Her mind was trying to tell her something. She rolled over quickly and examined the flooring. She chose one rectangular piece that looked as if it stood a little raised off the floor and began prising.

She longed for a nail file, or a pen or a comb, anything to slip under the taped, bound edges of the matting, but her handbag had been taken from her so she had to make do with her fingers. She broke off her nails and scraped the tips of her fingers, but one end of the mat was eventually up and Kitty hurriedly pulled it aside so that she could examine the floor underneath.

Noise floated up to her now, the clinking of china and the subdued hum of conversation. She must be directly above the restaurant. Kitty's heart lifted. If she could drop down into the restaurant surely she would be safe? Even if the staff was part of the gang, some of the customers must be ordinary members of the public. They wouldn't dare harm her in front of witnesses and she could phone for the police.

There would be enough space between the solid joists of the floor to squeeze her body through. Over the dusty surface of what must be the top side of the ceiling of the restaurant ran a tangle of electrical cables. Kitty leaned down and pushed them aside and tested the surface she had to break through. It looked like some kind of board panelling that had been nailed to the flooring joists. But how was she to break through it?

Kitty sat back on her heels to consider the problem. There was nothing in the room she could use to break a hole in the surface. Whatever other rules of society Wing Fat Lee might break, everyone still took off their shoes before entering his living space. Kitty didn't even have her shoes to use as a hammer. Her thoughts broke off as the metal door to the room flew open.

A very angry Wing Fat Lee stood in the entrance. Despite the fear that gripped her throat, Kitty leaped to her feet and jumped as high into the air as she could. There was no time now to try to break safely through the ceiling of the restaurant. All she could do was land on the spot with as much force as she possibly could and hope that her weight would carry her through.

It was amazing how much time she had to hope — hope that Wing Fat Lee wasn't carrying a gun; hope that none of the electrical cables that snaked through the floor cavity were live; hope that she was heavy enough to break through; hope that she had judged her position correctly and wouldn't land on one of the solid joists.

Then Kitty's feet touched the surface and there was a confused bounding as she landed on the hard board that was both the floor of her prison and the ceiling for the restaurant below. For a moment she thought it was going to hold.

She jumped again. With a rending, splintering noise, the surface split. At the same time, the nails that had held it up against the beams tore out, popping as they went.

★　★　★

Kitty felt herself sliding, slowly at first and then with increasing rapidity, through the dusty, narrow hole she had created and down into the restaurant below. She landed dead in the middle of a low, polished wood table. Clouds of acrid smelling dust flew about her, and splinters of wood dropped around her.

Bent nails tinkled to the ground.

Winded, she lay still on the table top for a moment, listening to the screams and exclamations of the party of Japanese men who had been sitting on the low cushions around the table. Their dark suits were now splashed with spilled food and wine, and streaked with dust from the broken ceiling.

Kitty, still dazed by her fall, sat up and looked around her. Other diners in the restaurant, spooked by the crash, had jumped to their feet. Some were trying to get closer to see what had happened. Some, perhaps under the impression there had been a bomb and might be another, were struggling for the door.

One enormous chef, dressed in white, was brandishing his long sharp knife as though he were looking for the enemy! Suddenly there was a crash and a ferocious crack by the entrance to the restaurant, followed by clouds of acrid smoke.

I didn't cause that, Kitty thought dazedly.

Dark-clad figures streamed in through the doors and windows of the restaurant. They leaped purposefully through the chaos. Some raced upstairs. Others tackled the knife-wielding chef. Others herded the innocent diners out into the fresh air.

Kitty sat frozen in the middle of her table with her mouth open. Bulky in his bullet-proof vest, a soldier ran over to Kitty. He was in anonymous black combat gear from head to toe and his face was covered by a black balaclava and goggles, but Kitty knew who it was. She looked up at him mistily.

'Max! Oh, Max!' she said.

The black figure stripped off its headgear and she was staring up into a familiar pair of brown eyes. Max gathered her up in a crushing embrace. Then he shook her hard.

'Kitty! Are you all right?'

'I was until you shook me,' she protested, laughing up at him.

Max's face softened, but he shook her once more.

'Don't you ever scare me like that again!'

He could never tell her the nightmares he had lived through on his way to the restaurant.

Kitty laid her hand on his arm.

'Max, were you still having me followed?'

'No.'

'Then how did you know where to find me? I thought you would go to the Lucky Dragon Club.'

Max gathered her up even closer to him.

'I nearly did,' he admitted, 'but somehow I got over being stubborn enough to trust you and your sources of information.'

Kitty peeped over his shoulder into the restaurant. She was very happy to see Wing Fat Lee handcuffed between two black-clad marines. She suddenly registered the sheer scale of the operation.

'Goodness, Max, how many of you heroes are there?'

His grip tightened.

'The whole team's here.'

Kitty tipped back her head and looked into his treacle-toffee eyes.

'Max! You got all those soldiers out because of me? Because of my pendulum?'

She was deeply touched to think of Max risking so much because he trusted her, and her way of going about things. With a happy sigh, she reached up and kissed his cheek gently.

'Max, thank you for believing in me. And Max, I can tell you where the missing weapon component is. That's what Wing Fat Lee was after.'

A relieved smile curved Max's lips.

'Oh, Kitty, I'm so glad I eventually listened to your intuition! I couldn't have borne it if — '

Overcome by emotion, he couldn't finish his sentence. He wrapped his arms around her and hugged her tightly.

She pushed him back and complained, with a laugh in her voice.

'Do you think you could take off your bullet-proof vest before you crush me?'

Max reached for her lips. He punctuated his words with loving little kisses.

'You deserve crushing. You deserve kissing to death. You deserve a better husband than me, but, oh, Kitty, will you marry me?'

Her whole heart was in her eyes as she smiled up at him.

'Oh, Max! I'd love to! But I'd be a terrible army wife.'

'You'd be an incredible army wife.'

Anxiety clouded Max's face.

'You might have to put your career on hold because I move around so much. But, Kitty, did you know that we can retire from active service at thirty-five? If you can only wait until then, we could open a flower shop together.'

Kitty reached up and smoothed away the crease between his brows.

'I'd love to go into business together.'
She smiled. 'I don't mind waiting a little.'

Pure happiness shone from Max's eyes.

'It's a deal! We'll go shopping for a ring tomorrow.'

Max bent his head to kiss her again, but he was interrupted by a loud cough from behind.

'Hey, Max, don't you want to see what we've found? This is it all right! We'll nail Wing Fat Lee and the gang for life with the evidence we've got here.'

'Later! You all know what to do. I've got more important things on my mind right now.'

And this time he refused to be distracted. His lips came down on Kitty's with tender, loving firmness. She feebly tried to push him away.

'Max, maybe you should go. You have to think about your career,' she insisted.

'My career doesn't come first. You do.'

Emotion deepened his voice.

'I can't believe how close I came to losing everything. I would never have forgiven myself if I'd been too late to save you.'

Kitty couldn't resist pointing out that she had nearly escaped by herself by the time they arrived, but she softened her words with a kiss.

'I underestimated you all along,' Max admitted. 'Looks like you have a lot to forgive me for.'

Moved by the genuine contrition Kitty heard in his voice, she hastened to put her arms around him.

'None of that matters now,' she said lovingly. 'Not now we understand each other.

Max met her gaze with a brilliant answering smile and then pulled Kitty into his eager arms. He glanced down at her blissful face.

'And now, darling, you are going to see what it's like when the military takes over.'

Laughing happily, Kitty surrendered to his loving embrace.

We do hope that you have enjoyed reading this large print book.

Did you know that all of our titles are available for purchase?

We publish a wide range of high quality large print books including:
Romances, Mysteries, Classics
General Fiction
Non Fiction and Westerns

Special interest titles available in large print are:
The Little Oxford Dictionary
Music Book, Song Book
Hymn Book, Service Book

Also available from us courtesy of Oxford University Press:
Young Readers' Dictionary
(large print edition)
Young Readers' Thesaurus
(large print edition)

For further information or a free brochure, please contact us at:
Ulverscroft Large Print Books Ltd.,
The Green, Bradgate Road, Anstey,
Leicester, LE7 7FU, England.
Tel: (00 44) 0116 236 4325
Fax: (00 44) 0116 234 0205

CONVALESCENT HEART

Lynne Collins

They called Romily the Snow Queen, but once she had been all fire and passion, kindled into loving by a man's kiss and sure it would last a lifetime. She still believed it would, for her. It had lasted only a few months for the man who had stormed into her heart. After Greg, how could she trust any man again? So was it likely that surgeon Jake Conway could pierce the icy armour that the lovely ward sister had wrapped about her emotions?